AN AFTERLIFE OF REALLY CREEPY STORIES

Edited by
Dean Wesley Smith

Stories from Pulphouse
FICTION MAGAZINE

An Afterlife of Really Creepy Stories

Published by WMG Publishing Inc.
All stories reprinted from the pages of
Pulphouse Fiction Magazine
Cover and interior design copyright © 2024 WMG Publishing, Inc.
Cover art copyright © by PenWin | Depositphotos

ISBN 13 (Trade Paperback): 978-1-56146-997-0

MORE FROM PULPHOUSE

PULPHOUSE FICTION MAGAZINE SUBSCRIPTION

Available in eBook and Paper subscriptions

Go to **www.pulphousemagazine.com**

- 6 Monthly Issues in eBook
- 6 Monthly Issues in Trade Paperback
- 12 Monthly Issues in eBook
- 12 Montly Issues in Trade Paperback

PREVIOUS PULPHOUSE ISSUES

Go to www.pulphousemagazine.com to buy any of our previous issues, including the very first Issue Zero!

MORE STORIES FROM *PULPHOUSE FICTION MAGAZINE*

A Twist of a Knife

Alibi Murder

Aliens Among Us

Cattitude Edited

Destination Tomorrow or Yesterday

Don't Touch My Magic!

Ghosts Among Us

History Repeats for No Reason

Implode the Membrane

Jingle My Bells

No Way: Totally Twisted Tales

Run!! Creatures, Critters, and Pulphousers...

Snot-Nosed Aliens

That's Really Messed Up

There'll Be Blue Popcorn Without You!

Three Sheets to the Wind

Twisted Robots, Oh, My!

STORIES FROM THE ORIGINAL PULPHOUSE

Stories from the Original Pulphouse: A Fiction Magazine

Stories from Pulphouse: The Hardback Magazine

ALSO BY

DEAN WESLEY SMITH

COLD POKER GANG

Kill Game

Cold Call

Calling Dead

Bad Beat

Dead Hand

Freezeout

Ace High

Burn Card

Heads Up

Ring Game

Bottom Pair

Case Card

THE POKER BOY UNIVERSE

Poker Boy

The Slots of Saturn: A Poker Boy Novel

They're Back: A Poker Boy Short Novel

Luck Be Ladies: A Poker Boy Collection

Playing a Hunch: A Poker Boy Collection

A Poker Boy Christmas: A Poker Boy Collection

Dry Creek Crossing

Hot Springs Meadow

Green Valley

SEEDERS UNIVERSE

Dust and Kisses: A Seeders Universe Prequel Novel

Against Time

Sector Justice

Morning Song

The High Edge

Star Mist

Star Rain

Star Fall

Starburst

Rescue Two

CONTENTS

AN AFTERLIFE OF REALLY CREEPY STORIES

INTRODUCTION

DEAN WESLEY SMITH

This anthology by its very title could easily have been just a book filled with three authors.

R.W. Wallace does a fantastic ghost fantasy detective series set only in the same cemetary and I have published a bunch of her wonderful stories and have more coming.

Robert J. McCarter is also a master at his ghost stories and I could have easily included four or five of them in these pages.

And then, of course, Kevin J. Anderson with his fun Dan Shamble Zombie Detective character. Talk about a perfect fit for *Pulphouse Fiction Magazine*.

And with the title of this anthology.

But alas, I set a rule for myself (that I wanted to break a few times) that I could only use one story per author per book.

And then I set a second rule for myself that I didn't want to use a story that had already been in another one of these fun anthologies. Nineteen of them before this one.

Yeah, I know… way too many stupid rules. But I lived by them fairly easily because *Pulphouse Fiction Magazine* is so full of great stories in the 30 issues so far, there was not a shortage to go over, that's for sure.

However, I almost had two zombie stories, sort of... Kevin Anderson's wonderful zombie detective character, and a story that is in the most recent issue by Annie Reed called 'Throw the Zombies from the Train." I love the story and really wanted to pretend it fit here.

But Annie's wonderful story "After" fit better, so you are just going to have to read her zombie story in issue 30. So only one zombie story. After all, I am the editor and I make the rules..

Or so I tell myself. Hope you enjoy the stories.

Dean Wesley Smith
Las Vegas, NV

LIVE THE PULPHOUSE LIFE!

Grab your Pulphouse mug and fill it with your favorite beverage and lounge in your coziest chair with the Thumper pillow while you read the latest issue of *Pulphouse*.

Want to mark off the date when your next issue will arrive? Get the *Pulphouse* calendar featuring some of our favorite *Pulphouse* cartoons!

Find all this and so much more at the *Pulphouse Fiction Magazine* online store at:

http://pulphousemagazine.com

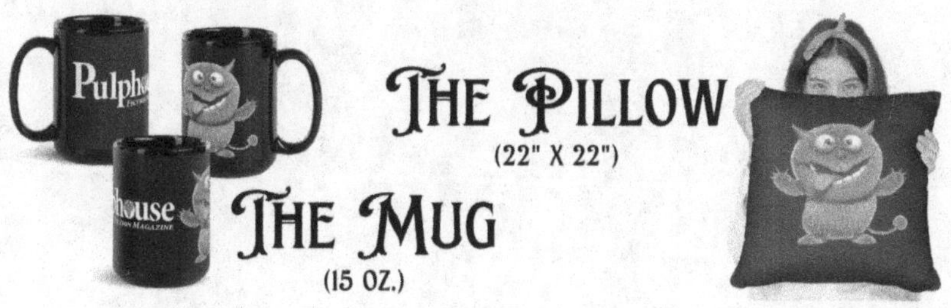

And say hi to Thumper while you're there.

HARRY THE GHOST PIRATE

ROBERT J. MCCARTER

Robert J. McCarter gives us a wonderful, heartfelt story in his ghost world series. I love these stories and always love putting them in issues. I think after you read this one, you will as well.

Robert has published seven novels and his short fiction has appeared or is forthcoming in The Saturday Evening Post, Fiction River, Andromeda Spaceways, Inflight Magazine, *and numerous anthologies.*

Look for more of Robert's work at his web site https:// robertjmccarter.com/

HARRY THE GHOST PIRATE

ROBERT J. MCCARTER

We've got a new ghost at the graveyard. His name is Harry, and he likes to dress up as a pirate, complete with eye patch, peg leg, and a green parrot perched on his shoulder.

It's annoying. The silly clothing and all the clomping around and saying "Arrrr," and "Matey," and "Shiver me timbers."

I mean, I get it. The mortal coil has been "shuffled off," so why not play at pirate while you studiously avoid your unfinished business that keeps you an earthbound spirit.

I get it, but it's annoying. But I guess my modus operandi is to complain about other ghosts while studiously avoiding my own unfinished business.

And I will admit I am a bit jealous that he can pull off a pirate so effectively. I mean, underneath the dreadlocks and behind the eye makeup, it's still Harry with his round, pasty face and his dull hazel eyes. Make that *eye*—the patch, you know. Holding a form that foreign and that complicated is just plain hard for any ghost to do.

Take me. I'm still wearing the simple white nightgown I died in. I can't hold another form to save my afterlife. Different ghosts are good at different things, I totally get that, but this girl would love to wear some jeans, maybe some Jimmy Choo heels, a nice glittery silk top. And maybe lose about twenty pounds. No, make that thirty.

But no, Harry is off annoying everyone as a pirate, and I am just chubby Drew in her nightgown with mousey brown hair that hangs halfway down my back and plain brown eyes. Now that I'm dead, I really shouldn't care about how I look, but I do. Biology has a way of sticking with you even when it's years gone.

Harry has been talking about finding gold lately. He's a pirate, right, so this is a logical progression. Clichéd pirate costume? Check. Annoying pirate speak? Check. Screeching parrot? Check. What's left, except to go in search of some gold?

But we are in Tucson, landlocked in Arizona. No ships to sail, no islands to explore. So, silly me, I thought the quest for gold would dry up then and there. I mean, it didn't look like Harry had found anyone to join him on his quest, and to my great relief, no one else had changed their ghostly form to look like a pirate.

"Ahoy there, me fine lass," Harry said one summer's night in the graveyard. He had clomped slowly across the green grass, dutifully and arduously maneuvering around the gravestones with his peg leg. Slow going. Something of a method actor, you might say.

"Hi, Harry," I said, trying to keep my face straight. I don't know a lot about history, but I know the Hollywood-style, clichéd pirate Harry was portraying bore little resemblance to reality. I don't think it was actually very fun being a real pirate.

"Ya might'a heard, but I'm lookin' ta assemble a crew of fine hardy mates to go in search of gold."

I nodded.

"Gold!" the parrot screeched. And I must admit, Harry had done a good job with the parrot. Its feathers looked totally real, and when the bird squawked, Harry's mouth didn't move. They guy had true talent when it came to manipulating his form.

"Oh. I . . . Are you asking me to go with you, Harry?"

"Aye. That I am." He paused and looked around, as if preparing to share a secret. "I hear told that you, Miss Drew, are a fine witch and can transport us instantly anywhere."

Okay, so I'm a witch in Harry's pirate world. Yeah, that doesn't bother me. Around here, it's called "popping" when a ghost goes from one place to another, instantly. Some ghosts are good at it, and some can't do it at all. I'm very good at it. As long as I can visualize the place, I can pop there.

"So, no ship? I thought you were looking for a crew?"

"Aye, lass, I am," he said, leaning toward me. "But I aim to find the Lost Dutchman's Gold Mine out in this here desert. It has riches beyond a mortal's ability to imagine, and since we aren't mortal anymore, I think we should be the ones ta find it."

I stared at him. Harry used to be an accountant. Now I don't know what an accountant's job is actually like, but it sounds super boring. Maybe Harry just loved pirates and, finding himself dead, he just went for it. Or maybe he's not quite all there, and this is the best he can do to cope with being dead.

"Yeah," I began, "but since we aren't mortal, we don't need the gold."

Harry stood up straight and took a deep breath. No, ghosts don't breathe, but many of the biological tics still stick around with a similar purpose.

"No, lass," he began, his face serious. "We don't need the gold, but me sister does. Her wee one is got the scourge, the cancer, and the bills are threatenin' to pull her family down to Davy Jones' locker."

"Need the gold!" the parrot squawked.

I blinked. Another one of those biological holdovers.

Everyone in the graveyard knows how you died. It's how you introduce yourself. Like me, I say, "My name is Drew, and I died of uterine cancer." Or Harry, he says, "Ahoy! Me name is Harry, and the scourge of bladder cancer broadsides me and drug me down to the depths like a hungry kraken."

Thus the blinking.

Not only had we both died of cancer—yeah, yeah, there are a lot of us like that here—but his niece was facing it, and he felt helpless to do anything about it.

Maybe that explained the whole pirate thing.

"Okay, Harry," I said with a nod. "You've got yourself a witch."

He smiled wide and suddenly looked fifteen years younger.

"All hands on deck!" the parrot squawked.

"We set sail at first light," Harry said.

———

One thing that follows you into the afterlife is the human ability for self-deception. Reality is still hard to see clearly, even when you are a lot less real than you used to be.

Earlier I mentioned my mousey brown hair and my extra thirty pounds and how I wanted to "lose" that weight. Even though I'm a ghost and it is quite literally not "weight."

And I might have given the impression that is what I looked like when I died.

It wasn't.

I had no hair and was skeletally thin.

I was thirty-seven when I died after several rounds of cancer. Started in the uterus and migrated from there.

Really, I should celebrate how wonderfully long my brown hair is, like it was when I was sixteen. I should revel in each extra pound, because keeping on weight was so hard to do for so long.

Your default appearance as a ghost is kind of like how you think of yourself. So I think of myself with really long mousey brown hair and thirty extra pounds.

And I don't like it.

Even though it's my own "default" appearance.

Even without the biology, we humans are complicated.

I mention all this because after Harry happily clomped away, I was again jealous of his marvelous ability to maintain his ghostly appearance, and then I meditated on my own twisted dislike of my own internal view of myself. Which made me wonder what dichotomy Harry was holding close. What reality of his own could he not see?

Sometimes we fool ourselves and we know it. Sometimes we fool ourselves and we have no clue.

It's the latter that concerns me.

It happened to me when I first got sick. I had crap energy (life is busy, right?) and unexplained weight loss (yeah!) and put off going to a doctor for far too long. Might have had a different result if I had done something about it sooner.

All that rumination aside, I had committed to go looking for gold with Harry.

He came clomping up right before the sun rose the next morning. I was on the wing of some old fighter jet in the aircraft boneyard at Davis–Monthan Airforce Base. I had a good view to the east—dead airplanes, dried grass, distant buildings, and the low hills hunched on the horizon.

A ghost in an airplane graveyard has a kind of poetry to it, right?

When I saw Harry, I felt bad and hoped he hadn't clomped all the way here from the graveyard. That would have taken the rest of the night, but the guy was committed to his pirate thing.

"There you are, me lass," he growled, sounding tired.

"Sorry, Harry. I didn't mean to make you walk all the way out here." Except maybe I had. Maybe I had been testing Harry, seeing if he knew me well enough to know where I liked to greet the new day.

"Not another thought. A cap'n will walk a long mile for his crew."

I smiled. There may be nothing at all realistic about his pirate thing, but it was starting to grow on me. I looked around. "Where is the rest of the crew?"

He sighed and shook his head, and the parrot screeched, "Cowards!"

And then it hit me. Harry was just another lonely ghost who didn't fit in with any of the other groups. Something else we had in common. I turned away and watched as a spark of light ignited on the horizon, a pinpoint of yellow taking on the darkness.

We watched the sun lift itself above the craggy hills, slowly, resolutely, the ordered rows of old, discarded planes glinting in the new light.

Harry wasn't one of those ghosts who has to fill every moment with talking and that boded well for our journey.

"Where to, Harry?" I asked once the sun was fully above the horizon.

"Well, I been thinkin' on that, lass, and I'd like you ta use your potent magic and sail us to the top o' Weaver's Needle. We'll have a mighty good view there, and it is said that the shadow of the spire points ta the location of the gold."

I nodded. Weaver's Needle is deep in the Superstition Mountains east of Phoenix and rises to a high, sharp point out of the surrounding cactus and mesquite bushes. I haven't been there, but I've seen pictures of it.

I grabbed Harry's arm, a careful bit of business since I had to match the frequency of my ghostly form to Harry's, and popped us there so we could start looking for gold.

———

The tip-top of Weaver's Needle is hard tan rock and a few hardy bushes and grasses. It's narrow and maybe a hundred feet long and twenty feet wide. This is rough country, dry desert dominated by cactus, prickly pear and some large Saguaro, with lots of scraggly mesquite bush.

The view is spectacular—rough, rocky ground rising and falling sharply. Weaver's Needle is nearly sheer for four or five hundred feet and then the broad cone around it becomes full of folds in the rock like the ground is a badly wrinkled blanket.

I sucked in a breath of surprise when I saw it. The sun was still low, most of the land in shadows, the high rock we were on brightly lit, turning the tans more orange.

I was a bit off when I popped us, so we were about twenty feet above the rock. Not bad for never having been here. I still had hold of Harry's arm, so I floated us down.

"Harry, this is . . ." I didn't have the words.

"Aye, Drew. It be spectacular. A right fine ship you've landed us on."

And I could see it. The rock was long and narrow, almost like it was a keel and the massive ship had capsized and was under the rocky waters below.

"What now?" I asked.

He took a deep breath. "Well, we search, lass. Every last nook, every last cranny. We follow the shadow, and we find the gold."

I nodded and didn't speak any of my doubts. Like how people had been looking for the Lost Dutchman's Gold Mine for more than a hundred years and never found it. It's kind of a tourist thing now.

We watched the sun drive out the darkness and watched the shadow of Weaver's Needle slowly become more defined to the west.

"What's her name?" I finally asked.

"What?" Harry said, sounding surprised with not a bit of a pirate accent. I mean it was just one word, but he didn't call me "lass" or "arr" it up at all.

"Your niece, the one we need the gold for. What's her name?"

His hazel eye flicked to mine, and I wished I hadn't asked. He looked so sad. "Her name is Megan, and she's the most beautiful and perfect thing I've ever seen."

I bit my lip as hard as I could, but of course that kind of thing doesn't hurt. A whole sentence without the accent and his parrot had stopped moving, looking suddenly like a stuffed animal.

"How bad is it?" I asked.

"It's bad, Drew." Coming from someone who lost his battle with cancer, it made me think Megan wasn't going to be alive much longer. He blinked back tears, another one of those biological things we still do.

I wanted to ask more, like what kind of cancer, what the grade was, how they were treating her, but I didn't. Harry wasn't really here to find gold. He was here to keep himself from worrying about his niece.

Whether he was fooling himself about this or not, I didn't know, and it didn't matter. Gold wasn't what this girl needed. It wouldn't save her. But it was what Harry needed.

"Avast ye!" I said, pointing to the west where the shadow of Weaver's Needle was just starting to come into focus. My pirate voice was just awful compared to his. "That there shadow is right clear enough now. Let's sail forth and find the gold!"

"The gold!" the parrot squawked, looking alive again.

Harry smiled at me, but it was a bitter little thing, like he had something sharp in his mouth.

I took his arm and popped us to the shadow's edge.

———

We searched for three days.

I mean, it wasn't a bad way to spend our time. In the gorgeous folds of rock, safe from the heat (because you're dead), and no need for food or water (because you're dead). And when you're dead, it's good to have something to do.

Harry talked like a pirate.

When he started to lose it, I talked like a pirate.

We looked in every nook and cranny we could find, ranging pretty wide from the shadow's tip.

Harry would clomp along on his peg leg and I would fly and cover as much ground as I could. When the shadow moved a ways, I would go grab Harry and pop him to the new spot.

At one point, Harry said, "It's a right fine thing that you can fly, me witch."

I smiled at him and nodded. I didn't worry about him when he was fully in character.

We found mesquite and sagebrush and cactus (so much cactus), ants, rabbits, coyote, a few hikers, and even a couple small caves. But nothing that would indicate a mining operation. No caves large enough. No signs of earth having been moved. Nothing.

At night, we would sit atop Weaver's Needle and talk until the stars were a glittering field of diamonds above us. We would mostly talk about pirate stuff, like hidden treasure and seeking new horizons and being outside the reach of the law, which I could appreciate. We were ghosts. We were constantly exploring new ways to spend our days and live our afterlives, and we were, quite literally, outside the reach of the law.

After we ran out of piratey things to talk about, we rested.

Ghosts do need some rest, and there is this form of sleeping called "fading" where you're just gone for a while. How long you are gone and where you show back up is a bit unpredictable, so neither of us did that. We were just quiet and let time slip by.

It's either like a pleasant meditation or a terrible nightmare, depending on how close to the surface your regrets are.

And let's face it, you don't end up an earthbound spirit with obligatory unfinished business without some regrets. Make that a lot of regrets.

Harry's nights were not good.

I would hear him moaning and crying like he was in terrible pain. Sometimes he would call out names. Like Megan, his niece we were trying to find the gold for. Or Anna, his wife who he left behind. He and Anna never had kids, so I could see how Megan would be real important to him.

And I have my own stuff. Like my fiancé, Binu, and how my paranoia that he was going to cheat on me chased him away. How I had never had kids—something else Harry and I had in common. And the cancer, always the cancer. I'm three years dead and the trauma of it still comes knocking.

As a ghost, your regrets can really get you. There is this place called the "bardo" that refers to a ghost who is trapped in regret until it has completely taken over and is their entire world.

I was clearly doing better than Harry. So, on the first two

nights, when it got bad for him, I would pretend to cry. I mean real epic, heartrending stuff. I had the material (and, really, who doesn't?), so I let it rip. I wailed there on the top of Weaver's Needle in the Superstition Mountains.

And it worked. Harry would shake himself out of his own nightmares and come check on me. Sit with me. Talk to me. We really got to know each other, and I am happy to say that Harry is quite human, imperfect as we all are, but very gentle and sweet.

But on that third night, it got bad. Real bad.

Back at the graveyard, we had this nightly gathering of the ghosts called "The Midnight Circle." Ghosts tell stories, put on shows, share. It can really help, but I guess Harry was too long away from it, because it was clear he was slipping toward the bardo.

I tried my wailing that third night, but it didn't snap him out of it. His pirate costume was gone, and he looked unkempt in a faded blue hospital gown, his face pale, his form way too transparent. When I saw that, I realized how much I missed the pirate get-up. I even missed the damn parrot.

His ghostly form was diffuse, like he was slightly out of focus.

Not good.

The common view of ghosts—wailing, moaning, inconsolable—is about those who have fallen into the bardo. And once there, it is nearly impossible to pull a ghost back out of it.

"All hands on deck!" I cried in my terrible pirate accent. "I had me a vision of gold, glitterin' gold."

Harry didn't even look at me. He was standing at the end of Weaver's Needle, on the highest point looking northwest. If he had been in his pirate garb, I would have said he looked like a captain on the prow of his ship, surveying the choppy waters ahead. In his hospital gown, he looked like someone on the top of a high-rise, thinking of jumping off.

And in some ways, that's exactly what he was.

I flew over to him and tried to grab his arm, but his form was so diffuse, I didn't dare try to match it. As a ghost, if you look human, you feel human, which was why Harry was always clomping around on his peg leg.

"Harry!" I shouted, no more pirate voice. "Come on, Harry, don't do this. We'll find the gold. I swear, we'll stay out here as long as it takes."

He still didn't look at me, his form getting more diffuse.

I considered popping back to the graveyard and getting help, but I didn't think he had that much time.

Harry no longer cared about gold. He no longer cared about being a pirate. What did Harry still care about?

"Megan needs you," I said gently. And as I said it, I felt it was true. Once the biology is gone, all us ghosts are more intuitive than when we were alive. "Right now, Harry. She needs you right now. I can take you to her."

He slowly turned his face to me, and the sadness there made me want to weep. Where was that annoying black eyeliner and eye patch? Where were the dreadlocks and pointy hat? Without them, with the sorrow filling him up, Harry was . . . Well, he was bardo bound.

He shook his head slowly and looked out over the moonlit desert. He took a shuddering breath and said, "They moved. I lost them."

It hit me, like I had been punched in the gut. Harry had been checking on his loved ones from time to time, like many of us do. It's not healthy to spend too much time with them;

the regrets will get you. When Megan was diagnosed, Harry was devastated. He spent some time away. He developed his pirate persona to compensate. When he felt strong enough to check in on them again, they were gone.

"Look at me, Harry," I said, putting as much authority into my voice as I could. "Look at me!"

He slowly turned his head, his hazel eyes barely focusing on me.

"I'm your witch, Harry. I can take you to her, but you've got to help me."

"You . . . you can?"

"Yes, Harry, I can. But I need you to come back to me. I need you to tell me what she looks like."

I was making promises I didn't know I could keep. Sure I could pop, all day long, but I had to be able to visualize where I was popping to. A place. A person. As long as I can see it, I can do it. But I had no idea what Megan looked like.

"She's the most beautiful and perfect thing you've ever seen," I said. "She needs you. Right now."

"Megan needs me," he said, his voice slightly stronger.

"Yes, Harry. And I need my captain."

He took a deep breath and nodded. It wasn't easy, it took time, but Harry slowly came back to himself, and soon he was peg-legged and parrot-festooned and telling me all about Megan.

How she loved to dance and how she hated carrots. About her adorable lisp and how long it had taken her to start talking. About her beautiful brown hair and bright blue eyes. About their trip to Disneyland when she was five. About the horseback riding lessons she had been taking before she got sick. How Harry and her used to love to play pirates.

And then I could see her.

And then I popped us to her.

And then things got really difficult.

———

The room in the hospice house was cheery, with lacy blue curtains and pastel blue walls, but it was dominated by a hospital bed and a wisp of a ten-year-old girl lying in it. Her parents were there, wane and exhausted, slumped in chairs, Megan's mother holding her hand and crying softly. Her father had his head in his hands and wasn't moving.

Megan was too thin and her brown hair was gone and tied on her head was a red bandana. My nonexistent stomach fell, and I wanted to run away, and fast.

Megan was dying.

I looked at Harry, expecting to have to battle him back from the bardo again, but he was still fully pirate, his look grim but resolute.

"Ahoy, Megan!" he said, stepping into the bed so he could be close to the girl. "It's your uncle, Cap'n Harry, and I've come ta take ye on a fine adventure. Me crew and I have been searching for the Lost Dutchman's Gold Mine, but we can't find it. We need ya, lass, and your fine weather eye."

It was still and silent in the room. Too silent. I noticed Megan's chest wasn't moving. We were too late. She was gone.

"What do you say, lass?" Harry said. "Will you join us?"

I couldn't move. I couldn't speak. I felt terrible for Megan, for this family. Their grief would be huge. And maybe Megan had moved on, maybe she didn't have unfinished business.

But if she hadn't moved on, if she was a ghost, I felt terrible that we hadn't gotten here in time.

But then Megan stirred. Well, not her body, that was done, but her spirt stirred, and she slowly rose up out of the biology that had failed her.

"Uncle Harry?" she asked, her voice high with surprise.

"Aye, lass. It's me."

"Am . . . am I dead?" she said, looking around at her parents. Her ghostly form had beautifully long brown hair, but she still wore the red bandana. Her body was not skeletal anymore but was a healthy weight.

"Aye, you are. As am I. But it ain't so bad." He stepped back from the bed and stomped on the floor. "Look! I finally got me a peg leg!"

Megan giggled. "Can I have a peg leg?"

This was a delicate thing Harry was doing. Many ghosts go bardo right away. Kids especially. It's a lot to deal with.

"Aye, you can. I can teach ya how. But we must go, lass. There is gold ta find." He extended his hand to her as she floated further from her spent body.

She blinked and looked at her parents again, then down at the frail body she was floating above, her face contorting in grief. "But, Mom and Dad . . . I . . ." Her form started going diffuse along the edges, and I knew we would be in trouble soon.

"Megan," Harry said, his pirate accent gone. "It's me. It's Uncle Harry. I know this is confusing, but come with us, and I'll explain everything. You'll see your parents again. I promise."

Megan sniffed and nodded and took her uncle's hand.

It's been almost three months, and we're back on Weaver's Needle, the stars strewn above us, our search done for the day. Sure, the sodium glow from Phoenix to the south and west spoils it a bit, but looking north, there are more stars. An ocean full of them.

Captain Harry the ghost pirate was there in his tattered buccaneer's shirt, his parrot on his shoulder. Next to him was his first mate, Megan, with her tricorn hat and her glorious long brown hair flowing down her back. She's gone a bit nontraditional, choosing to wear a frilly white dress, although she does have a peg leg to match her uncle's and proudly clomps around after him.

We've had some tough times with her. Adjusting to the afterlife is not for sissies, but things have slowly gotten better. Being pirates in search of gold has helped. A lot.

We are a crew of six now, with three other ghosts having joined our search for the Lost Dutchman's Gold Mine.

I am still the witch of the crew, popping us all over the Superstition Mountains. And since I'm the witch, no one cares that I'm still in my nightgown and my beautiful long brown hair is not covered by a hat. Right after we first met, Megan said, "You and I have the same hair." And since her hair is glorious, and no one would ever call it mousey, then my hair is beautiful too.

"Gather 'round, me hearties," Harry called out.

Our new crewmates are Marge and Kyle, an older couple with gray hair and broad smiles, and Benjamin, a nice young man with beautiful brown eyes who died in a traffic accident. I could be fooling myself, but I think he joined the crew because of me.

"I know we been searching long, and we been searching hard," Harry said, "with not one bit o' gold to be seen. But take heart. The desert is vast, and there are more legends for us to chase, more treasures for us to look for."

There was a murmuring of assent. I find the desert beautiful, and it's just fine with me if we never find a thing.

"We aren't just a crew," Megan added, standing tall and proud. She took her uncle's hand and squeezed it. "We are a family."

Harry and Megan reached out their hands, and we all formed a little circle. Six ghosts holding hands at midnight atop Weaver's Needle. A half-dozen earthbound spirits with something to do and someone to do it with.

Not a bad way to spend your afterlife.

And that, me hearties, is the real treasure.

NEW BEGINNINGS
R.W. WALLACE

This original story is in a series of wonderful fantasy mystery stories from R. W. Wallace that has been and will be in many of issues of this magazine.

These stories are not like any standard mystery. The detective is a ghost, limited to his own cemetery helping other ghosts move on by solving their problems. In other words, the detective is locked in a confined space with no tools, trying to help a victim discover what happened to them.

A wonderful series that I am lucky enough to run in this magazine. And for even more of her work, check out her website at http://rwwallace.com/

NEW BEGINNINGS
R.W. WALLACE

Everybody dies alone, they say.

No matter how surrounded you are by family and friends in your life, no matter how rich or poor you are, no matter your social status, we're all equal—and alone—in death. Nobody can walk that path with you.

I don't remember my own death, so I find it hard to argue the point, facts in hand.

But I don't like to think that whoever came up with that saying was right.

I can't speak for what happens at the exact moment when someone dies, but I *can* tell you that none of the people who come through our cemetery as ghosts are ever alone.

Clothilde and I are always here to help them adjust to being ghosts, and to help them move on once they've settled whatever unfinished business made them linger.

If either of us ever moves on without the other, whoever remains will, indeed, be lonely. It's something I don't think about all that much anymore—we've both been here for over thirty years, after all. Chances of either of us figuring out what we need to move on tomorrow are, quite frankly, slim.

It's been the two of us for such a long time, I've come to think of ghosts as belonging in two groups: us and them. Clothilde and I are the constants. The others are only passing through.

When other ghosts come through, we make the effort to get to know them. But we keep a distance, one that we need for our own well-being.

The first years in our cemetery, I befriended most of the other ghosts. Got to know them. What they liked, their sense of humor, their tastes and opinions.

And then they moved on, and left me behind.

Only Clothilde stayed.

So even though the rebellious twenty-year-old with wild, curly hair and worn Converse doesn't seem like the likely friend of a balding thirty-five year-old washed-out cop, we're the closest thing either of us has to a family.

We're *us*.

And together, we welcome new ghosts—while keeping the required emotional distance.

Today, I think we have a new arrival.

I say *think*, because the signs aren't as clear as usual.

When someone has unfinished business and becomes a ghost, they wake up inside their casket sometime between the ceremony in the church and the moment when the church doors open. Without much surprise, when someone wakes up and discovers they are stuck in a sealed casket, they panic.

Usually, they scream—*we* scream, I was no exception—and pound on the casket, trying to get someone to save them.

This is what alerts us to new arrivals. The large wooden

doors to our little stone church squeal open, the mourners pour out and wait on the small area in front of the church, huddling under shared umbrellas if the weather is as wet and depressing as it is today, and then the casket is carried out. Accompanied by screams if the person has become a ghost.

I *think* someone's yelling—but with the murmurs of the large group, the staccato *plops* of rain on umbrellas and gravestones, and the ringing of the church bells, I just can't be sure.

I can't even rule out the possibility of the yells coming from one of the mourners because the rain, the umbrellas, and a large number of hoods make all the people look blurry. This winter has been as depressing as they usually are in this part of France; rain, gray skies, and more rain. Every single day. Not even a single snowflake to brighten things up for a moment or two.

Now that it's finally March, maybe we'll get some sun and fresh spring.

"Is it possible to be too lazy to panic properly when you die?" Clothilde perches on the headstone of her own grave, her feet swinging back and forth, passing through the stone as if it weren't there, her head cocked as she listens for the yells.

"Maybe the rain muffles the sound," I say without conviction. I'm sitting on the small mound marking my own final resting place, very happy that ghosts can't get their pants wet, or feel the cold.

"The rain doesn't muffle ghost sounds," Clothilde replies but without her usual snark. She's too focused on the casket.

Biting her cheek, she stretches her neck, as if that would help her see anything better from across the cemetery. "I think it's someone old. All the young people are clearly family. If anybody is a friend, they're at least eighty."

That information is probably not be *quite* right. Clothilde may have been on this earth for over fifty years—twenty as a normal girl and thirty as a ghost—but her capacity for estimating the age of someone over forty leaves something to be desired.

But as I get up to get a better look myself, I have to concede the point. None of the "friend" mourners are a day under seventy.

"Let's get a little closer," I say and start walking toward the hole where the casket is to be buried. It's an existing grave in one of the old and fancy parts of the cemetery. The granite slab was removed yesterday to prepare for today's funeral.

I take the narrow paths winding past the gray tombs, glancing at some graves with fresh flowers and regretfully noting the ones that haven't been cleaned in several decades.

Clothilde follows behind while cutting a few corners. She was never one for following the rules of the living when it doesn't suit her. The grave of Monsieur Lopez she cuts through on purpose, like she always does when going through that zone. He spent some time with us as a ghost. Clothilde did not like him.

The burial in itself is pretty straightforward so I don't even bother listening to what the priest says. I go down to crouch down on the casket six feet under to make sure that the sounds I'm hearing are coming from inside.

Polite knocking and the occasional, "Hello? Does anybody hear me?"

Well, that's new.

"Definitely a new arrival, and a polite one at that," I tell Clothilde as I join her in the crowd of mourners.

"There's something weird about this death," Clothilde

says. She stands in the middle of the crowd, her hands on her hips, and studies everyone in the vicinity. "And there's something weird about the mourners."

I take the time to look, too. She's right. There's something off about the people around us—but I can't put my finger on what it is.

"What do you mean, there's something weird about the death?" I ask. "From what I understand, the woman was seventy-three, and her husband died and was buried here ten years ago." I find it highly unlikely that the newly arrived Madame Priaux was a murder victim, for example.

Clothilde moves toward a lone woman in her thirties standing somewhat apart from the group in the back. Tears are streaking down her face and this has clearly been going on for a while. Her cheeks are as wet as her raincoat, making it look like the hood has no effect whatsoever.

Clothilde scrutinizes the woman from head to foot several times. "They're too upset."

I fight the urge to roll my eyes—that's usually Clothilde's favorite way of expressing herself. "People are allowed to be upset when they lose someone they love."

Frowning, Clothilde leans in so close to the woman that their noses almost touch. "Not this much. Not for a woman in her seventies who's 'joining her husband.' Not for people who have already lost grandparents, so they know what it's like." She leans back and meets my gaze. "They're shocked this woman is dead."

I make a quick tour around the people present. And conclude that Clothilde is right.

"Maybe it's a familial or cultural thing. They don't deal well with loss?"

Clothilde's reply is a snort. At least she didn't roll her eyes.

The ceremony finished, people mill towards their cars. The young, sad woman remains, and is joined by a man who might be in his early forties. His hair is thinning on top and completely gray around the ears. His beer belly strains his coat around the waist and his black umbrella only covers his front. The back of his jacket is soaked, as are his legs from the knees down.

"Come now, cousin," he says to the woman. "No need to beat yourself up. You did the best you could. It was her time." He holds the umbrella away with one arm and reaches out the other toward the woman's shoulder, clearly to lean in to kiss her cheek.

The woman steps away. "Don't! I might have it."

The man sighs. "You didn't have any symptoms while you were with Mamie for a week, you haven't had any since she died. You're fine. Let me give you a kiss and some human contact. *That* is what we need when we're mourning."

The woman doesn't seem convinced but her cousin doesn't give her much choice. He leans in and kisses her cheek, then retreats back under his umbrella.

"Come," he says to her. "You need to get out of the rain. Can't have you catching your death in this weather." He guffaws at his own joke.

"She died from some kind of contagious disease?" Clothilde says when the two cousins leave the cemetery. "What, like, the flu?"

I can only shrug. We're in France, a country with health care for all and mandatory vaccines. I have to agree with Clothilde. The flu is the only common contagious disease I can think of that would kill an elderly lady like this.

"If that was the flu, then I'll eat a rat," says a shaky voice from behind us.

We rush over to the grave, and find an elderly lady with curled gray hair and thick-rimmed glasses with rhinestones along the top staring up at us, hands on hips.

"Would either of you young people mind telling me how I get out of this pit?"

———

Her name is Marie-Pierre and she's seventy-three. She used to be a teller in a bank, something she took a break from for fifteen years to raise three children, and eventually went back to when she started feeling claustrophobic in her own home. She has seven grandchildren, one of whom is in great danger of making her a great-grandmother very soon if she doesn't watch out.

"So how did you die?" Clothilde asks. Marie-Pierre didn't feel comfortable sitting on someone else's grave and her own isn't really an option right now, so we've settled on one of the benches under the plane trees. Clothilde is sprawled on the wet ground, ignoring the rain completely, her jeans-clad legs stretched long and arms propped behind her for unneeded support. I'm on the bench with our new colleague, keeping a polite distance.

Marie-Pierre waves a hand in the air. "Some kind of virus. I think. I was quite out of it when they took me to the hospital and although I know they talked about whatever it was around and over me, I didn't really listen." She gets a faraway look and the wrinkles on her forehead deepen. "I was too busy fighting to breathe."

We sit in silence for a while. I have more questions for Maire-Pierre but we're hardly in a rush. She was surprisingly quick to come out of the casket, which might be linked to her age. At some point, people know the end is coming, so it's easier to accept when it happens. Not that seventy-three means a foot in the grave. Rather…well, death is closer than it was yesterday.

"I don't suppose Noël is around?" Marie-Pierre twists around on her bench, scanning the cemetery.

That's the name that was already on the grave Marie-Pierre was buried in. "Was he your husband?" I ask.

"Yes. He died ten years ago. Heart attack from doing too much sport after he retired." She sighs and smiles wistfully. "My mother always told me he was stupid."

"I'm afraid we're the only resident ghosts at this time," I tell her. "Not everybody becomes a ghost, you see. And those who do, don't always linger very long."

Her sharp gaze, too serious for the ridiculous glasses she wears, catches mine. "Yet you've been here for some time."

"Yes. I have." I leave it at that. "Your husband never became a ghost. He must have moved on directly, like the majority of people do. He must not have had any unfinished business."

"Not other than getting up that mountain on his brand new bike," she grumbles. She glances at Clothilde, then back at me. "You are insinuating that I *do* have unfinished business? That's why I'm here?"

Clothilde sits up, wrapping her arms around her knees. "Do you know what it might be?"

Marie-Pierre takes her time thinking about it, cocking her head left and right, grimacing and mumbling to herself.

Finally, she shrugs and folds her hands in her lap. "Nope. Not a clue."

———

We expect Marie-Pierre to get visitors once the grave is sealed. Quite often, the people our ghosts have unfinished business with come back, because it's a two-way street.

For two days, not a soul comes to visit—not Marie-Pierre nor anybody else.

On the third day, we get another funeral.

With another new arrival.

This time, there's no doubt. As the church doors open, the screams blow out of the church, loud and male and angry. The pounding on the casket is constant and with several different kinds of resonance—this guy is hitting with both hands and feet. Today, miraculously, there's no rain, so we hear everything perfectly.

"Oh, my," Marie-Pierre says as she slips her glasses down her nose to study the spectacle over their rim. I've tried to explain that she doesn't need glasses anymore, and certainly shouldn't have trouble with focusing on something far away, but the woman just shrugged and adjusted her glasses.

Some habits are hard to kick—and some we don't want to.

We watch from afar as the casket is carried to a newly dug grave in the north-east section and the priest makes a quick sermon.

"Not too many people this time," Clothilde comments. She has abandoned her usual perch to stand on the other side of

Marie-Pierre, her arms crossed across her chest and a slight frown on her face.

"Huh," Marie-Pierre says as she yet again lowers her glasses to look at the mourners. "That *is* odd."

"Why?" I ask. We're supposed to be the specialists on funerals and mourners here, not the new arrival.

She points a bony finger at the family standing closest to the grave. A woman in her late fifties and two twenty-something men. They're all blond and stocky.

"That's Lisa and her weird sons. If Didier isn't with her, it means he's the one int the casket." She cocks her head. "Yes, that definitely sounds like Didier." She sends me a look that I'm unable to decipher. "Didier is one of the village's three doctors. He was *my* doctor."

She stops talking but the conversation is clearly continuing in her head. I also see her counting out the number of mourners and mumbling names.

"Everybody loved Didier," she finally says. "He was loud and smart and funny. The entire village should have come to his funeral." She waves at the twenty-five people huddled around the open grave. "This is only family."

I meet Clothilde's gaze over Marie-Pierre's head but my friend just shrugs at me. Village chatter doesn't interest Clothilde.

"Did his family get along well?" I've suddenly realized what seemed odd to *me* about this group—and I think it was the case during Marie-Pierre's funeral, too. "They're not standing very close."

Usually, during a funeral, people huddle close together, seeking human contact.

"They're the closest-knit family I've ever met," Marie-

Pierre says, her voice flat. She's realizing something's not right.

She puts a hand on my forearm, either to get my attention or to get that longed-for human contact that is forever denied us ghost. "What's going on?"

"I don't know," I reply, my voice serious. "I hope Didier will be able to help us figure it out."

Didier emerges from the grave two days later. By then, three new graves have been dug in the southern quadrant of the cemetery and I have a bad feeling in the pit of my stomach that won't go away.

"I can't believe this," are the first words out of his mouth as he crawls out of the grave. "Totally unacceptable." He's a tall man, completely bald, and at least twenty kilos into obese territory. He looks to be in his early sixties.

He catches sight of Marie-Pierre. "Oh, hello Madame Priaux. You're here, too, are you?" Finally free of the dirt, he straightens and stretches his back, then frowns as he realizes this doesn't have its usual effect on his body.

Ghosts don't get back pains—and we can't enjoy a good stretch.

"I'm Robert Villemur," I say, not wanting to wait for the man to ask the questions. "And this is Clothilde. Do you know what's going on? What was your cause of death? That of Marie-Pierre?"

I almost add the three empty graves but decide against it.

Didier gives me a once-over but he doesn't ask any questions. It may appear that if Marie-Pierre is working with me, then I'm okay.

"There's a new virus," he says. "Spreads like wildfire. Attacks the lungs. Especially dangerous to the elderly and those with pre-existing conditions."

He stares daggers at his bulging belly, as if it is the cause of his demise.

"What…" I trail off as I don't even know what to ask him. And even if a killer virus in the world of the living would be a disaster, I'm naturally more turned toward its effect on our ghostly world.

I've talked quite a bit with Marie-Pierre these last couple of days and I cannot figure out what her unfinished business is. If we don't know what the problem is, we can't solve it, and we can't send her off to the other side.

I hold up a hand, palm out. "I want to hear more about this virus, Monsieur, but I have one other pressing question first. Do you happen to know if you have any unfinished business with the living which might be keeping you from moving on?"

"Moving on." Didier turns in a circle to take in our little cemetery. "You mean this isn't the final stop?"

"Next to last," Clothilde says from her perch on a nearby mausoleum. "The one where you can tie up those last loose ends."

Didier nods a greeting to Clothilde. "Mademoiselle. Didn't see you there."

"From what I've understood, Didier," Marie-Pierre says as she pushes her rhinestone glasses up her nose. "Ghosts only linger when something is keeping them back. Finding the person who murdered them, speaking to a loved one one last time. Apologizing to estranged family members. Personally, I can't think of anything, but then my mind isn't what is used to be, so maybe I've forgotten?"

"That doesn't seem likely," I hasten to reassure her.

Didier shifts from foot to foot, his forehead creased into a giant frown while he considers the question. "Can't really think of anything." His voice is soft. "Wouldn't mind seeing my family again, but they know I love them. Got along with everyone. And it wasn't a person who killed me, it was this blasted virus."

Could their unfinished business really be with the virus? How is that supposed to work? How can a group of ghosts in a cemetery fight something as intangible as a virus?

I look toward Clothilde but her gaze is turned in direction the parking lot.

Two hearses just arrived.

———

"It's the Moulins," Didier says. There's a fatality to his tone that makes me think he's not surprised to see this particular family.

As the two caskets are pushed toward the church, three other cars arrive, with five people in each car. I assume they're the living members of the Moulin family. They vary in both shapes and sizes, ages and color. One of the men in the last car, a man who must be well past fifty, has a dry cough and leans heavily on a man I assume to be his son as they follow the caskets.

"You're not supposed to come out if you're sick!" Didier yells at the man. "Protect the rest of your disease-ridden family, man!"

Didier faces me, fire in his eyes. "What are the rules here? They can't hear me, I suppose? Can I touch? What can I do?"

"They can neither see, hear, or feel you," I say. "And you can't leave the confines of the cemetery. But sometimes their subconscious *can* get our messages. So it's always worth a shot, but it takes patience."

Didier is studying me a lot closer, all of a sudden. "Have we met?" he asks, frowning fiercely. "I didn't catch your name."

"Robert Villemur," I reply.

"The cop," Didier says. "I remember when you went missing."

My eyebrows shoot up and if I'd still had a beating heart, it would have sped up considerably. It's the first time another ghost has recognized me, in all my thirty years in this place.

I'm not buried with the rest of my family. I've never had visitors. I don't even have a proper tombstone, just a slight bump in the grass next to Clothilde's grave.

I have no idea if anybody who cares even knows I'm buried here.

I'm about to say as much when my attention is drawn to the two new caskets. "They're not going into the church?"

The procession is almost all the way to the newly dug graves already, the Moulin family trailing behind. The priest, walking ahead of the caskets, and the funeral agents managing the caskets, are all wearing masks and plastic gloves.

"There's less chance of the virus spreading outdoors," Didier says before running toward the coughing man.

The rest of us follow at a more leisurely pace.

"The entire family has a tendency to attract all types of diseases," Maire-Pierre says in a low voice. "Diabetes, high blood pressure, pneumonia, cancer. You name the disease, one of the Moulins will have it. Every time I went to Didier's office for an appointment I would meet at least one of them."

Didier is speaking directly into the ear of the man with the cough, trying to convince him to stay away from his other family members. He also yells at the whole group to keep their distance.

When the two caskets are lowered into the ground, Didier comes back to join us. "It's Gérard and Claude," he says to Marie-Pierre. "Two elderly brothers," he adds for my benefit. "The fathers or uncles to most of the people here."

We watch in silence as the priest holds his sermon at the graveside instead of inside the church. I'm fascinated to participate in this part of the funeral for the first time since my own demise. Usually, we only get the last words once the casket is in the ground.

I learn something new, too: ghosts wake up when the mass is over. Everybody echoes the priest's "Amen," and the yells start.

"Gérard! Where are you? What is going on?"

"Claude? Where am I? Why is it so dark?"

Clothilde glances up at me and curls her upper lip.

Two more ghosts.

———

For two weeks, we continue down the same slippery slope.

Six more funerals, six more ghosts—and fewer and fewer mourners attending the funerals.

We've received the coughing man from the Moulin family,

and the overconfident cousin from Marie-Pierre's funeral, the one who insisted on kissing the cheek of the woman who'd spent time taking care of the sick Marie-Pierre.

Marie-Pierre was devastated to discover he'd died—and then proceeded to give the man the talking-to of a lifetime for taking such a big threat so lightly.

For the last funeral, the final journey of one Mathilde Joubert, the thirty-six year-old cashier at the local Lidl, only her mother shows up to say her goodbyes.

When Mathilde crawls out of the grave four days later, there are twelve ghosts waiting for her.

I've sat down with all our new arrivals over the past weeks, digging into their histories and reasons for becoming ghosts. With the possible exception of a man who hasn't seen his children in over a decade, I find no unfinished business we need to settle, no reason for all of them to linger.

Except the virus.

But what can I possibly do about this thing from the confines of our cemetery? What could I do even *outside* of the cemetery? I don't know how to defeat a virus. I don't know how to bring it to justice.

When we go a week without any new funerals, I tentatively hope we've seen the worst of it. Eleven deaths within a month is a very high number for such a small village.

Eleven ghosts for eleven deaths has never happened—at least not in my thirty years.

Cothilde and I have started taking daily walks around the cemetery, just the two of us, to get away from the others for a while.

We've been used to it being just the two of us for so long, it's hard to adapt to having enough ghosts to make up an entire soccer team. So we take these walks, and pretend we're back to normal for a short hour every day.

"You think the gardener will be back soon?" Clothilde asks as we step through the growing weeds along the west wall.

I run a hand through the pale purple wisteria adorning the cemetery wall, wishing I could still smell their sweet scent. "The lockdown is apparently scheduled to end in two weeks," I say. "I'm guessing our gardener will be back then."

Right now, with nobody doing any kind of upkeep while the spring sun is shining beautifully, our cemetery is looking more and more abandoned by the day.

Or like an overgrown English garden.

I'm starting to think that nature gaining turf might not be such a bad thing.

Apparently, outside, the entire world has shut down, in order to stop the virus from spreading. Schools are closed, restaurants are closed, concerts are canceled, people are working from home… And everyone is sheltering in place, waiting for the plague to pass.

Yet in our cemetery, everything is the same.

Except for the growing weeds—and the twelve extra ghosts.

And the lack of visitors.

"We haven't had a single visitor since this all started with Marie-Pierre's funeral," I say. "Do you think that could be what sets them free? They need to say proper goodbyes to the people they left behind?"

Clothilde shrugs. "Except for that one guy, they don't seem to feel too strong a need to say goodbye. And for *all* of them to feel that way?" She trails off and jumps up to walk on the wall.

Well, she's walking on air right *next* to the wall—we can't cross the middle of the stone construction.

"I don't like having so many people here," she says as she carefully puts one foot ahead of the other, arms out for balance —as if there's any risk of her falling down.

"I know," I say.

Ironic, really, that we should spend so much time worrying about being all alone and then complain when we finally have company.

"The visitors should come back once the lockdown is over," I say. "Maybe we'll get some answers then."

And in the meantime, we'll try to pretend to be extroverts and enjoy the new company.

——————

Mid-May, under a beautifully clear and blue sky, with the sun shining down on the living and dead alive, the lockdown is lifted.

Everybody gets visitors on the very first day. Clothilde and I were feeling crowded with twelve extra ghosts—now add in hundreds of live visitors.

Clothilde turns into a gloomy teenager and follows some of the louder visitors around, telling them to be quiet and testing their sensibility to ghosts to determine if there is any point in attempting a prank.

I leave her to it.

I decide to join Marie-Pierre at her grave when her daughter comes with a bouquet of orange roses.

"They're from the garden," the middle-aged woman says. "You always seemed to love to come visit when that rose bush was in bloom." She looks to be in her fifties and is wearing a pair of washed-out jeans and a simple black t-shirt. Her hair is short and has dark blue highlights.

Marie-Pierre caresses her daughter's cheek with the backs of her fingers. "I loved to come visit any time." Her hand goes to the blue streaks. "When did you do this?"

The daughter must be sensitive to ghosts because her hand goes to her hair. "I got so bored during the lockdown," she says with a wistful smile. "Figured a little color in my life wouldn't hurt."

Marie-Pierre seems happy.

But she's not fading. Seeing her daughter again and having the chance to say goodbye is clearly not going to be enough for her to move on.

Someone seems to be causing a scene near the parking lot.

At first, I figure it's the live people—they outnumber us at least one to five, after all—but then I realize only the ghosts are reacting. Marie-Pierre is lowering her glasses to look toward the noise, and I see Didier straightening from where he was crouching next to a young girl at his own grave.

It's the beer-bellied cousin.

"What is that idiot Vincent up to now," Marie-Pierre says under her breath as she pushes her glasses back up her nose.

"Looks like he's not happy with his cousin," I say. "The woman who cared for you before you died?" I think that's her coming through the main gate right now and even though I can't make out the words, the anger and fury in Vincent's voice carries and clashes with such a beautiful sunny day as he hovers over her and yells straight into her face.

I rush to the poor woman's rescue but Clothilde gets there before me.

We might not have physical forms but we remember how things used to work. So when Vincent receives Clothilde's angry eyes right in front of his own face, he takes a step back.

"*What* is you problem?" Clothilde hisses.

The live woman draws a shaky breath and runs a hand down her face but she keeps moving, toward Marie-Pierre's grave if I'm not mistaken.

"What is my problem?" Vincent is not backing down from Clothilde and even goes to far as to try to push her away.

His hands go right through her.

He recovers quickly, though. "My problem is that I'm dead because of that woman. She had the virus and gave it to me and now I'm dead!"

"That's hardly fair, Vincent," Marie-Pierre says. She has joined us by the main gate. There's an entire area that the living are currently avoiding, though none of them will realize it's because there's a fight between ghosts going on.

Marie-Pierre shows she has learned to master the rules of being a ghost as she stands on thin air to get right into her grandson's face. "If she had the virus, it was because she caught it from me. Does this mean you are blaming me for your death?"

"Well...no, of course not," Vincent stammers. "It's not like you gave it to her on purp—"

"Did she go out of her way to give it to you? Cough into your face? Touch your hands?"

I see the moment Vincent thinks he's found a way out. "At your funeral, she—"

"She told you not to get near her," I say. "And yet you insisted on kissing her cheek anyway."

He sputters some more, until he realizes there's now a total of ten ghosts surrounding him, and not a one who seems likely to take his side.

Finally, he mutters, "So you're saying it's *my* fault."

Marie-Pierre tuts at him and pats his cheek. "It's nobody's fault, Vincent. *C'est la vie.*"

I can tell from her expression that Clothilde wants to point out that it's actually death, but luckily, she refrains.

————

As the cemetery is closed for the night, all the ghosts gather around Marie-Pierre's grave. Being the only one buried in an already existing grave, she's the only of the new arrivals with an actual tombstone, albeit still without her name on it. Some are sitting on the large slab of granite covering the tomb, others are standing on the path. Clothilde is perched on a neighboring headstone.

I'm off to one side, arms crossed and feet wide. I know the stance is a little aggressive but not figuring out what everybody needs is getting on my non-existent nerves.

"Did everyone get visitors today?" I ask the group and they nod or reply in the affirmative with expressions ranging from grinning to worried frowns.

"Yet nobody moved on." I tried making time for everyone throughout the day, to listen in on their "conversations" with their loved ones, but still, nothing jumped out as an obvious reason for lingering.

With one notable exception. "Vincent," I say, "I think if you can forgive your cousin for giving you the virus, or accept your part of the responsibility, that might be enough."

After a quick glance at the glaring Marie-Pierre, he mumbles, "There's nothing to forgive. It was nobody's fault."

Right. Now what?

As the last sunlight disappears below the horizon, we sit in silence. I'm all out of ideas and cannot even imagine what living in this cemetery will be like if we're going to be thirteen instead of two.

"It's a beautiful night," Marie-Pierre comments. "So odd, that the world keeps turning without us."

"All my patients will have to find a new doctor," Didier says.

"Our kids are going to fight over those houses we own together for decades," Gérard says and his brother Claude nods.

"My cousin is going to feel guilty about my death forever." Vincent hangs his head.

"So the world keeps turning," Marie-Pierre says. "But not quite the same way."

"A worse way," Vincent says.

"Nonsense." Marie-Pierre's voice has lost its wistfulness. She's dead serious. "It's different, not worse. This virus has changed the world. But change isn't always worse, or better. It's different, and new."

"And it will be different and new without us." Didier's words could be taken as depressing or fatalistic, but his tone is anything but. It sounds like he's made a happy discovery.

Like a responsibility has been lifted.

He throws out his arms to indicate the cemetery around us. "We have a new world to discover. Together."

The mood shift for the entire group comes slowly, but clearly. They're letting go of the anger at having died from some invisible virus they had no control over. They tell each other how happy they are to see that their living relatives seem to be safe and doing well.

And they plan ahead. As a group.

I walk over to stand beside Clothilde. "I think they're planning to stay," I say low enough that none of the others will overhear.

"Over my dead body." Then Clothilde throws her head back and cackles a loud laugh.

When she calms down, she pats my shoulder. "Don't worry, it won't come to that." She lifts her chin toward the group of ghosts. "They're already leaving."

She's right.

In a large group on the path now, they're slowly becoming transparent. Didier notices first. "What does this mean?"

"You're moving on," I say.

"You're not," Marie-Pierre says.

I shrug. "That's all right. You take care of each other."

Excitement and fear cross their faces as they fade. They grab each other's hands mere seconds before they all disappear.

Silence.

Night has fallen but we can somehow still see each other.

"Wanna go hang out on my grave?" Clothilde says as she jumps down from her perch.

"Always." I follow slowly, reclaiming my cemetery and taking my time to enjoy the return to normal.

And sending up an extra thanks for having my friend here with me.

See? Nobody is alone in death.

THE EYEBALL AT THE END OF THE RAINBOW

KEVIN J. ANDERSON

Kevin J. Anderson keeps writing these really fun and original Dan Shamble Zombie PI Adventures. Of all the ongoing characters being published these days, Dan Shamble fits Pulphouse the best.

Kevin has published more than 140 bestselling novels and with his wife, bestselling writer Rebecca Moesta, founded Wordfire Press.

Kevin is known for Star Wars, X-Files, and Dune novels, as well as his many original science fiction novels. But back in 2012 he started something a little different for him, a series of humorous horror mysteries featuring Dan Shamble, Zombie P.I.

I love the fact that we have Dan Shamble in Pulphouse.

THE EYEBALL AT THE END OF THE RAINBOW

KEVIN J. ANDERSON

I

At Chambeaux & Deyer Investigations, we take every client seriously, no matter how ridiculous the circumstances might seem. As a zombie detective in the Unnatural Quarter, I never know what might show up next.

So, I greeted the distressed leprechaun with a professional demeanor and an interested smile, tilting my fedora to cover the bullet hole in my forehead. The short, spritely figure entered our offices, weaving noticeably as he led a blind, hulking centaur.

I'd heard of mixed marriages before, but I'd never seen such a striking example of mixed mythologies.

The leprechaun wore a traditional emerald jacket, jaunty cap with a prominent shamrock, and a fat black belt with a big silver buckle. His hair and beard were shockingly red, and he looked as if he were about to break into a jig, though he seemed inebriated and unbalanced.

Like an Irish seeing-eye dog, he guided an eight-foot-tall cyclops of the Harryhausen variety, with a pointed horn like a lonely antler on his bald head. He had a bare muscular chest and warty, knobby shoulders. His crooked teeth might have been prominently featured on any "before" poster for basic dental services.

His face had one prominent but empty eye socket, like a fleshy crater. Resting one hand on the leprechaun's shoulder, the cyclops strode in with misplaced confidence and bashed his shoulder on the side of our door. "Are we here yet, Bailey? Or did you stop at a pub again?"

I extended my grayish hand in greeting, though the cyclops couldn't see and the leprechaun seemed distracted. "Welcome, gentlemen," I said. "I'm Dan Chambeaux, zombie private investigator, and you've come to the right place."

I had no idea where they were trying to go, but my ghost girlfriend Sheyenne says we should always make potential clients feel welcome.

At her receptionist's desk Sheyenne glowed with ecto-plasmic greeting and wafted up from her chair. I may be the unnatural detective, but the blonde ghost always steals the show. "At Chambeaux and Deyer, we're prepared to look into any matter, natural or unnatural," she said. "Dan provides zombie detective services. If you prefer *human*, our partner Robin Deyer can offer legal services on monster matters."

"Oh, it's the detective services we'll be in need of," the leprechaun said in a rich brogue that was enhanced, or slurred, from a little too much Irish whiskey.

"We need to find my eye!" said the cyclops. "Tell him, Bailey. Is he there?"

"Sure, and he's right in front of you. He can tell it's the eye that's missing!" The leprechaun turned to me with a toothy grin. "I am Bailey O'Cream, and this here is my associate, Ulysses S. Clops."

"He's my sponsor," the cyclops growled. "And he lost my eye."

The leprechaun looked embarrassed. "Ulysses and I serve as each other's sponsors, help each other out, have each other's back, as it were."

Robin Deyer emerged from her office, eager to help. "Sponsors for what?" She's a beautiful, professional African American woman in her mid-thirties with a passion to prevent injustices against unnaturals. She was accompanied by Alvina, a cute-as-a-button little vampire girl, my half-daughter. The kid wore a fuzzy pink unicorn sweater, and her blonde hair was in a pair of bouncy pigtails.

Seeing the leprechaun, Alvina squealed with delight. "I've seen him on my boxes of Unlucky Charms!"

"Oh dear," said Bailey O'Cream, blushing until his cheeks matched the color of his beard. "'Twas one of my early sponsorship endorsements, and it's embarrassed me ever since." He sniffed. "Myself, I'll say no more about it."

"It drove him to drink," said Ulysses.

After making introductions, we got to the basics of the case. "Sponsors for what?" I pressed again.

"Err, well, I'll tell you it's a kind of support group. UTI would be what we call it—Unnatural Total Inebriants."

The cyclops grunted. "For monsters who want to go on benders responsibly."

Although I frequented the Goblin Tavern, my zombie metabolism and the formaldehyde in my bloodstream prevented alcohol from having much effect on me.

I could see Robin's disapproval. She rarely drank anything but green tea or club soda with lime. "These benders—are they a regular occurrence?"

Both the cyclops and the leprechaun shook their heads. "Oh dear, oh dear!" Bailey said. "Not at all, you see. They're only for special occasions."

"Only on Catholic or Jewish holidays," said Ulysses.

"So, a regular occurrence then," I said.

The cyclops's shoulders slumped. "I drink with Bailey, but I prefer to use giggle weed myself—the very best marijuana strains. Less of a hangover."

"Himself, he likes to pass the days stoned as could be," the leprechaun said.

The cyclops blinked his empty eye socket, which I found very disturbing. "Yeah, stoned. It reminds me of when I would stand on a cliff and hurl big stones down at those pesky Greek ships."

"Greek ships?" Robin asked. "But your name is Ulysses, the Roman variation of the Greek Odysseus. Don't you mean Roman ships?"

"Doesn't matter. I never hit any of them anyway. Poor depth perception." The cyclops scratched the warty skin on his left shoulder. "I still like to get stoned, though."

"He's happy to imbibe in my Irish whiskey when I share, so," Bailey said. "And that's all to the good, since I have a magic whiskey bottle that refills itself. The drinks are always on me."

"Can I pour some of the whiskey on my Unlucky Charms?" Alvina asked. "I want to see if it turns red like milk does."

Robin, Sheyenne, and I all answered the little vampire girl

simultaneously. "No."

I still didn't understand what mystery these two wanted me to solve. "Let me get this straight. As sponsors for Unnatural Total Inebriants, you two watch over each other and make sure neither one gets in trouble."

"It's designated nondrivers that we are," said the leprechaun. "Best that way."

"But something went wrong," the cyclops said.

"As it usually does on repeated benders," I said, trying not to sound judgmental. "Did Mr. Clops trip and poke his eye out with a stick?"

Both the leprechaun and the cyclops reacted with horror. "No!" Bailey said. "Sure, and I'd be failing as a sponsor, then." His brogue thickened as he grew more upset.

Robin had taken out her yellow legal pad and her spell-bonded pencil, which was ready to take notes all by itself. "Then how did Mr. Clops lose his eye?"

Ulysses muttered in his deep voice. "*I* didn't lose my eye. *Bailey* did."

The leprechaun scuttled forward, wringing his hands. Ulysses followed, still gripping the little guy's green-clad shoulder. "Now, it's not that I *lost* the eye, you understand, so much as *misplaced* it. We didn't want anything to happen to my friend's one and only eye, so we took precautions, don't you see? Removed his eye is what we did, and then hid it safely away in a secure place."

I tried to follow along, but I felt I was missing an important piece. "So…this cyclops has a detachable eye?"

The leprechaun tugged the front of his frock coat in indignation. "Now, sir, have you ever met one who didn't?"

I could honestly answer that I had not.

"And now the eye's gone missing!" said Bailey. "And it's you that we would like to hire to find it again, Mr. O'Shamble."

"It's pronounced Chambeaux," I corrected, knowing it was a lost cause.

"Where exactly did you lose it, Mr. O'Cream?" Sheyenne asked.

"Misplaced it, truly," the leprechaun insisted. "Even though I took precautions. Sometimes after a mighty bender, I have a bit of inexplicable memory loss, so."

"Inexplicable?" Robin muttered.

"So I wrote down careful instructions on where to locate the eyeball again. I'm not entirely unprepared, you know."

From the pocket of his green jacket he withdrew a folded sheet of paper, a Chinese takeout menu, on which a few words had been scrawled. The writing looked like the tracings of a heartbeat monitor from a werewolf undergoing a bad monthly transformation.

I looked at the menu, but the scrawl made no more sense to me than the Chinese letters did.

"I wrote down precisely where I stashed the eyeball," Bailey said. "Now we just have to go there and find it, you see."

"I can't see," Ulysses said, "but I know Bailey has terrible handwriting even when he's sober."

The leprechaun scoffed. "Ha! When have you ever seen me sober, Ulysses?" The cyclops had no answer for that. Bailey lowered his voice. "They're clear instructions."

"Clear instructions written in illegible handwriting," I replied.

Alvina tried her best, but even the little vampire girl couldn't decipher what the words said.

"So, will you take the case?" the cyclops asked. "Translate Bailey's handwriting and track down my eyeball."

"Of course we'll take the case." Sheyenne took the scrap of paper and studied the scrawled writing.

Robin interrupted in a no-nonsense voice. "Mr. O'Cream, are you willing to take care of Mr. Clops in the meantime? He's required to have assistance, thanks to the Unnaturals with Disabilities Act." She had helped pass that particular law, and she was very proud of the results.

"You got to take me to the dispensary, Bailey," the cyclops said. "I'm running low, and I don't want to get stressed."

"In good time, Ulysses, in good time. Sure, you still have plenty in your stash. Soon enough, these good people will read my handwriting and find your eyeball. Then all will be right with the world."

———

II

The cases don't solve themselves—that's my motto. And the leprechaun's handwriting didn't read itself either.

After Bailey O'Cream had led the blind cyclops away, suggesting they stop for a quick nip at the pub, I held the Chinese menu under a bright light so I could look for fine details.

Alvina, who was always helpful as my detective's assistant (for extra credit with her schoolwork at Nosferatu Academy) suggested that I had the paper upside down. I turned the menu around, but to no avail.

The vampire girl rummaged in her science kit and took out a large magnifying glass that would have made Sherlock Holmes the envy of Victorian society. Even enlarged, illegible handwriting was still illegible handwriting.

Meanwhile, Sheyenne dug into unnatural histories and guidebooks, brushing up on facts and figures related to leprechauns and cyclopes. (She discovered that detachable eyes were not, in fact, all that uncommon.) She studied leprechaun magic and lore to determine if the little guys had some secret language that we would have to decipher, old Irish runes or special calligraphy. Although their thick brogue could be incomprehensible, there was no specific leprechaunese.

No, this was just a case of criminally bad handwriting, and it was up to me and my team to decipher it. Ulysses S. Clops's monocular vision depended on us.

As a zombie detective, I know I can't do everything myself. I have a network of experts and confidants, both humans and unnaturals, who have knowledge where I have deficiencies. Since I have a lot of deficiencies, I know a lot of experts.

The Unnatural Quarter's foremost expert—and practitioner—of terrible handwriting was Dr. Zonda Nefarious, whose scribbled prescriptions were both renowned and feared.

Several years ago, a trio of shady gremlins who were seeing the witch doctor for persistent toenail fungus discovered that no pharmacist, apothecary, or alchemist in the Quarter could interpret Dr. Nefarious's writing, so they convinced an unwitting pharmacist that they needed the most expensive and dangerous controlled substances—with unlimited refills—which they sold on the black market.

In her defense, Dr. Nefarious claimed that medicine was not an exact science, nor was handwriting. If anyone could unravel Bailey O'Cream's penmanship, it would be the witch doctor.

Alvina and Sheyenne insisted on going along to the Brothers and Sisters of Mercy Hospital. It's not often that a little kid, vampire or otherwise, is eager to go to the doctor, but she loved the hemoglobin lollipops Zonda Nefarious gave her as a treat.

Sheyenne called ahead for an appointment on a "medical matter." We whisked past the hospital's front desk, but had to meet with Dr. Nefarious's physician's assistant Igor (who was no help at all because of his acute nearsightedness).

Finally, the witch doctor came in to see us, clucking her tongue. She had a stethoscope and a severed hangman's noose around her neck, and a medical chart tucked under her elbow. Like all witch doctors, Dr. Nefarious had bristly black hair under a pointed hat with stars and crescent moons. The significant wart on her chin indicated her status among witches.

Looking at me, the doctor noted the hole in my forehead, then she glanced at Sheyenne, but her gaze passed right through her ectoplasmic form. When she saw Alvina, though, she bent down and extended a gnarled finger to touch the kid's delicate baby-teeth fangs. Satisfied, she whipped a hemoglobin lollipop from the pocket of her surgical coat. "Here you go, dear. You need more sugar to take care of those little fangs." She clucked her tongue again. "Now then, what seems to be the matter?"

Sheyenne spoke up. "We need your help reading."

"Oh, reading problems?" The doctor looked at Alvina with immediate concern. "Does the dear child have undiagnosed dyslexia?"

"No, it's about a leprechaun client who suffers from incomprehensible autographia." I figured by speaking in a medical sounding language I could better get through to her.

"Ahh, sounds serious. Let me see."

I pulled out the folded menu and pointed to the scrawl. Dr. Nefarious studied it carefully, pulled out her ear probe and squinted through the lens, pointing the light down on the written clue. "It appears he crossed out an order of General Tso's chicken."

"I wish it were that simple, or that spicy," I said. "This message contains the whereabouts of a highly valuable object, and we urgently need a translation."

"Please help us," Alvina said. "If we can figure out the words, then we'll know how to solve the case!"

The witch doctor studied the whorls and loops, the scribbles and lines of Bailey's handwriting. "Ah, I think I see now. I'm familiar with this type of notation, though it's rarely used." She blinked her eyes. "And not often this badly."

"Can you make out any of it? Any words at all?"

"This one here..." She tapped the paper with a long, pointed fingernail. "I think it says...*Gold*. Yes, that is quite clear to me."

I saw nothing clear at all on the smudge of ink.

"And this appears to be *Pot*...I think. Who did you say wrote this message?"

"A leprechaun," I said, and the wheels were already turning in my mind.

Pot and *Gold*. We needed to find the leprechaun's pot of gold, and then we'd have the eye of the cyclops!

III

Although leprechauns are notoriously tightlipped about their hidden pots of gold—I knew that much from folklore as well as from the cute summaries on Alvina's Unlucky Charms cereal boxes—I decided the best approach was to ask Bailey O'Cream directly.

Chambeaux & Deyer needed to be paid for our services, but I wasn't in this for a pot of gold. I was looking for an eyeball. Maybe the leprechaun would make an exception, especially if his brutish friend and sponsor twisted his little green arm.

In our new client paperwork, Sheyenne had (legibly) written the address of Ulysses S. Clops. I decided to go see him and the leprechaun by myself, since Alvina had schoolwork to do.

The cyclops lived in a modest but homey cave that was part of a new cave development on the south end of the Quarter. All of the cave openings in the subdivision looked the same, though many were adorned with culturally specific decorations, windsocks, lawn ornaments, even a few pink flamingos.

With the luck of the Irish, I found a subdivision map at the entrance. Since I had the specific cave number, I eventually located the dank and dripping grotto where the two lived. The doorbell let out an incongruous series of Westminster chimes, and soon the spritely leprechaun wobbled to the door, half dancing a jig and half tripping over the uneven cave floor. He held the refillable bottle of Irish whiskey in one small hand.

"Well, if it isn't O'Shamble!" he said with a wide grin. "We hope you solved the case. Ulysses is getting intolerable." Then he frowned so deeply that his shamrock drooped. "Alas, I can see from the expression on your mug that you're not bringing us an eyeball."

"These things take time, Mr. O'Cream, but I do have a strong lead. I've managed to decipher your clue." Triumphant, I pulled out the folded Chinese menu.

Bailey doffed his stylish hat and gestured me inside with a bow. "Delighted to hear it! And next time, I promise I'll send my clues by text. That'll be more readable than handwriting, don't you know."

I wanted to tell the leprechaun and the cyclops at the same time. It wasn't exactly clear which one of the two was our actual client, and Robin was a stickler for legal details. I followed him into the central living grotto.

Holding his whiskey bottle, Bailey plopped down on a threadbare, plaid sofa that looked like free furniture left on the sidewalk for large trash day. Sitting on the opposite end of the sofa, the cyclops stared at me—actually, he turned his face toward me, but even without his eyeball, he didn't seem ready to see or hear anything.

"Better tell me the details, O'Shamble," said the leprechaun. "I've only had a few snorts, so I'm sharp as a tack. But Ulysses smothered his sorrows in a raft of reefer smoke, and now he's Blarney stoned, you might say."

"I have something to cheer you up, Mr. Clops." I raised my

voice, although increased volume didn't have any obvious effect on the well-lit cyclops.

Ulysses blinked his empty eye socket and flared his nostrils. "Where did Bailey put my eye? You better find it. He never should have lost it."

The leprechaun sniffed. "Once again, boyo, I didn't lose it. I kept it safe."

"You kept it *lost*!" the cyclops grunted.

I cut them off before they could get into an argument. "I consulted an expert with professionally bad handwriting, and she was able to interpret the clue. Now I know where the eyeball is. Mr. O'Cream, you hid it in your pot o' gold."

"My pot o' gold!" Bailey cackled. "That's only nonsense for the gullible. It's a myth that leprechauns have a pot o' gold!"

"You're just greedy," said Ulysses. "You've got my eyeball! Give it back—and some of the gold that you've been holding out on me."

I raised my hands. "Everyone says a leprechaun's pot o' gold is at the end of a rainbow, though I did plug that into my GPS without success. We'll need your leprechaun magic, Mr. O'Cream."

"A rainbow? And where do you think I'm going to find a rainbow in the Unnatural Quarter?" The leprechaun took a long swig of Irish whiskey draining half the bottle, though by the time he set it back upright, the amber liquid had refilled to the top again. "It's always cloudy and gloomy here, the way the Unnaturals like it."

Ulysses was growing more agitated. He picked up a fat, claw-rolled joint and inhaled deeply, holding the acrid smoke in his lungs. Even so, he showed no sign of relaxing. "You suck as a UTI sponsor."

Now the leprechaun flushed scarlet. "It's *you* I'm protecting you from, ya daft gimp. Sure, even when you do have your eye in its socket, you can't see how much I do for you."

"Ugh! What you can do for me is *turn around and leave!* You're evicted, and I don't want you as my sponsor anymore. I'll file a report with the local UTI chapter."

The leprechaun furiously stomped his heel on the floor as if he were channeling Rumpelstiltskin. "Aye, I'll leave—and good riddance to you, too. I'll share no more of my rare Irish whiskey. Go and get stoned all by yourself. You and I have bent our last bender!"

In defiance, the cyclops inhaled a huge breath of pungent smoke, then exhaled with lungs like blacksmith's bellows, choking both of us, even though I rarely needed to breathe.

Growing more enraged, Ulysses expressed his anger in a demonstrably physical fashion. He pounded on the cave wall and flung an ash-laden ashtray like a frisbee. I barely ducked out of the way, and the object only knocked my fedora askew. Then he grabbed the plaid sofa cushions and hurled them about. Now I understood why they looked so frayed.

Bailey and I made a hasty exit. "You'd better find your pot o' gold, and quick," I said.

"I'm giving out about that dolt and his eyeball! Or his sponsorship...or even his friendship." He sounded defiant, but also hurt. "I knew I should have brought my shillelagh and cracked it right on his noggin!"

"I thought all that marijuana would make him mellow," I said.

Bailey grunted. "That *is* mellow."

As we walked away, he offered me a snort of Irish whiskey, and I accepted just to keep the client happy.

———

IV

My regular watering hole was the Goblin Tavern, a place where everybody knew my name, but no one held it against me. Sitting with a beer, I could propose improbable solutions to the world's problems with the sarcastic and curmudgeonly Officer Toby McGoohan, my best human friend. By now, our usual barstools had been worn into the specific configurations of our buttocks. (Those are as distinctive as personal fingerprints—few people know that.)

McGoo was already there, dressed in his blue patrolman's uniform after a day of walking the beat. He had slurped a couple of inches of beer from the pint in front of him, nursing it on the fast track. "Hey, Shamble," he said.

"Hey, McGoo." It was the start of what would surely be another pithy conversation.

Francine, the hard-bitten bartender whose rough-and-tumble life had prepared her for rowdy customers—monsters or otherwise—started pouring my beer as soon as I walked in the door.

"It's nice to be known and liked," McGoo said, nodding to Francine.

She slid the beer over to me, and I smiled with gratitude as I replied to McGoo. "Or in your case, just *known*."

"Somebody's having a pissy day," McGoo said. "I was going to tell you a new joke, but now I'll hold off."

I heaved a sigh. "That does brighten my day."

He sounded sincere now. "Rough case?" I told him about the cyclops and the leprechaun and the search for the missing eyeball and the fabled pot o' gold. He responded with a grave nod. "Mixed mythology. Those cases can be tough."

"The two are mutual sponsors for Unnatural Total Inebriants. Their bond was strong before, but now I think it might be shattered."

"It's all fun and games until somebody loses an eye," McGoo said.

As if by magic, the tavern door swung open, and a small, green-clad figure bounded in, belting out a chorus of "Oh, Danny Boy." Bailey O'Cream was taking the drinking establishment by storm, at least a little one. He spotted me and strolled toward our barstools. "By my four-leaf clover, it's Dan O'Shamble!"

"It's just Shamble," McGoo said.

"It's Chambeaux," I corrected.

With some effort, and a little bit of levitation after touching the side of his nose, the little guy nestled himself on the barstool next to us. "It seems I am in need of new drinking companions, so. Have you two lads had your first bender yet?"

McGoo raised his eyebrows. "Had my first one of those back in police academy days."

"Then you're due for a whiskey!" the leprechaun observed.

I introduced the two of them, and Bailey was mollified when he heard the name McGoohan. They shared their Irish heritage, though the leprechaun seemed more intent on consuming Irish whiskey, but he had not brought his bottle with him. He loudly ordered the best Francine had to offer, and she came by to pour him a shot. Then another. Though he didn't have a magically refilling bottle, Francine did her best to keep up with his thirst.

Over time, Bailey grew more maudlin, and it was not an improvement. "You guys are the best drinking buddies ever!"

McGoo and I stuck to beer, and we wisely did not attempt to keep up with a proud member of Unnatural Total Inebriants.

"I miss my cyclops," Bailey moaned. "What am I going to do without the big guy? I didn't mean to misplace his eye."

"We'll find the eye," I reassured him, but if the leprechaun had no idea where to find his own pot o' gold—even when he was semi-sober—I couldn't even begin to look.

"He needs me," Baily sniffed. "Ulysses can't take care of himself, with or without his eye, don't you know? It's me who takes him to the dispensary, and myself, to be sure, who gets him home. I've never held it against him, but he partakes too much."

He slugged back another shot of Irish whiskey. "Did you know how many times I've had to stop him from running with scissors? And now I don't have a sponsor at UTI—and neither does he. Would you two fellows watch over me?" he asked in a plaintive voice, then dropped his forehead to the bar and fell into a stupor.

"Francine will," I promised. I paid my own tab and even bought McGoo's beers. But the leprechaun was going to have to dip into his own pot o' gold to pay for all that expensive Irish whiskey.

V

Bailey O'Cream was not going to be in any shape the next morning to help out in the investigation. In fact, I expected him to be in the tavern restroom bent over a pot o' porcelain and vomiting something emerald green.

I went back to the office for some heavy thinking. Usually, I prefer to do private investigating by wandering around the Unnatural Quarter. The cases don't solve themselves, but I might bump into just the right thing at the right time. Now, though, I refilled my World's Greatest Zombie Detective mug with offensive black sludge and sat behind my desk to ponder the mystery of the illegible clue.

How could I find a leprechaun's stash? It must be somewhere close and accessible, because Bailey had intended to give the eyeball back without any hassle. And neither the cyclops nor the leprechaun were the type to take long and complicated precautions when they were about to start one of their legendary Catholic or Jewish holiday benders.

Alvina bounced in and plopped herself on the chair on the opposite side of my desk. She nestled a bowl of breakfast cereal on her lap and slurped one spoonful after another. The Unlucky Charms had turned the milk—and her lips—a bright arterial red, as advertised. Her smile showed little white fangs. "This is helping me to think like a leprechaun," she said. "Do you want some?"

"I'll use my own methods, kid." I tapped my forehead, hoping that the answer would fall right out of the bullet hole there.

I took out the now-rumpled Chinese menu and stared at the scrawl, unable to see how Zonda Nefarious had deciphered either "pot" or "gold" out of that mess. "I need to find the pot o' gold at the end of a rainbow, but rainbows are rare around here."

"Maybe it's a metaphorical kind of rainbow," Alvina said.

I tried to think of a fabric store, or someplace that sold ribbons or flags, or even a Tibetan monastery with prayer reels and colorful banners. The Unnatural Quarter had a few fabric stores, but no Tibetan monastery that I knew of.

Sheyenne poked her head in, asking if I needed help, just as I had a sudden idea. "Spooky, does the Quarter have a Gay Pride parade? Maybe Bailey put the eyeball there somehow."

"Three so far this year, Beaux—Zombie Pride, Vampire Pride, and Werewolf Pride, but they were all last month."

Well, it had seemed like a good idea.

I continued to ponder, and that usually led to walking around. "I'm going to stretch my legs, keep the rigor mortis at bay. Maybe I'll think of something."

Taking my fedora and sport jacket, I left the office and strolled down the main boulevard. The day was gray and gloomy as usual, but the murk seemed to be thinning. The weather wizards had issued a vampire advisory that today's forecast might include patches of unexpected sun.

I considered starting at the cave subdivision and wandering in a widening circle, trying to follow the leprechaun's train of thought. Bailey had wanted to protect the precious eye from any hazards they might encounter during their bender, and he would have stored it in a place he could conveniently retrieve—but a place uncommon enough that he'd needed to write a note to himself.

Bailey O'Cream was not an imp of deep thought or unnecessary complexity. The eyeball had to be close.

I looked up in the sky and suddenly, in what should have been accompanied by an angelic chorus, a rainbow glimmered through the misty, drifting clouds—the full spectrum from red to violet. Roy G. Biv!

I stopped in my tracks, trying to remember the last time I had seen a rainbow in the Quarter. That must be a sign! Or a clue! Or a weather incident!

The arc of the rainbow seemed to terminate in the south end of the Quarter, near the new subdivision of cave dwellings where Ulysses S. Clops lived. Exactly as I had thought!

I ran, glancing at sky, but also watching my feet and careful to look both ways when I crossed a busy street. I can be a fast zombie when necessary. I felt like a fool from folklore trying to find the end of the rainbow in order to grab a pot o' gold. But this was work related.

Before I got halfway to the cyclops cave, the perspective shifted, and the rainbow seemed to end in a completely different part of the Quarter. So I changed course. Zombies can be relentless, if nothing else. I hurried off, still trying to find the rainbow's end.

Alas, by the time the rainbow faded, I had reached only the garbage dump, where the stench was decidedly unmagical. I still had no pot o' gold and no eyeball.

VI

Since I was in the neighborhood after chasing rainbows, I decided to check on Ulysses S. Clops. Maybe he would have some idea where I could find his former UTI sponsor's pot o' gold. The big brute had been wasted when I previously brought up the subject, and by now I hoped he had calmed down and sobered up.

When no one answered the Westminster chimes, I grew concerned—where would a blind cyclops go? I decided to venture inside (which was not difficult because the cave had no door). "Hello? Ulysses, are you here?"

I heard sniffling and sobbing ahead in the main living grotto. The air reeked with so much marijuana smoke that I wondered if zombies could get a contact high. "Hello?"

None of the mess had been cleaned up, and it was fortunate Ulysses couldn't see the household disarray he had caused. The cyclops hunched on the creaking sofa with his head bowed so that the sharp horn pointed at me. With both big-knuckled fists, he rubbed his eye socket, where the tears continued to flow.

"I got nobody," he blubbered, then turned his blank face to me. "Except you—but who are you? I can't see."

"It's Dan Chambeaux, Mr. Clops, and I'm still working on your case. We'll have your eyeball back if I could just learn the location of Bailey's pot o' gold."

"I need him to take me to the dispensary! That's my first priority. I used up my stash."

"Shouldn't your eyeball be your first priority?"

"I have immediate goals and long-term goals." His eye socket suddenly filled with hope. "Can you take me to the head shop?"

"Do you know the name of it, or the address?"

The cyclops shrugged his warty shoulders. "I'll know it when I see it."

"So…we won't be finding it anytime soon."

He lifted his head. "Did you happen to bring any Irish whiskey?"

The leprechaun had imbibed enough for a small army the previous night. "I thought you didn't care for the stuff."

"It reminds me of Bailey," the cyclops said. "And I smoked my entire stash just to make me forget. I depended on him for so much. Please?" He turned his head as if trying to echolocate me. "I'll put my hand on your shoulder and we can wander around the Quarter. Maybe we'll bump into the dispensary. It's my favorite one. I use it all the time."

I tried to withdraw. "I was hired to find your eyeball, sir, not be your caretaker. If I can just find the connection between that leprechaun and the end of a rainbow, then I'll know what his handwritten note means."

"But I don't have any friends," the cyclops sobbed.

My dead heart was heavy on his behalf. I thought of how often McGoo and I teased each other, but what would I do without my best human friend?

He clutched the tattered, plaid sofa cushion in a bear hug and buried his face in it. He reminded me of the leprechaun drowning his sorrows in the Goblin Tavern. Those two were made for each other, more than just UTI mutual sponsors.

I was more determined than ever, even though I had hit a

wall on the case. I wasn't sure I could solve the mystery of the illegible clue.

But I could solve this friendship. I knew exactly what I had to do.

———

VII

Somehow, I intended to salvage this oddball eyeball case. I had hope again, or at least more focus and less confusion. Getting those two back together as sponsors and friends would be a good thing—at least I could accomplish that.

Sheyenne had taught me much about the nuances of unnatural relationships, but I decided to handle it myself. Though my clients were a leprechaun and a cyclops, this was still a "bro thing."

Then I thought about bringing in in McGoo for moral support, especially if we had to knock some heads together. We could play good cop/bad cop...but McGoo didn't like to be called a bad cop, because it was too judgy, so I would go it alone.

Ulysses S. Clops was sure to be huddling miserably in his cave, bemoaning his lost leprechaun, his empty stash of medicinals, and his lost eyeball. And I knew exactly where to find Bailey O'Cream.

Though it was still early in the day, the little leprechaun was in the Goblin Tavern sitting on the same barstool. His jaunty black hat and its shamrock rested on the bar top. He must have left and returned, because now he had his magically refillable bottle of Irish whiskey. He poured himself another shot and slammed it back with a sigh. "Magically delicious."

"I'm still charging you for those, you know," Francine said in her raspy, cigarette-smoke voice. She had stacked chairs on the tables to sweep the floor. "This isn't a bring-your-own-bottle party."

"But, lass, I did bring my own bottle."

"There's also a surcharge for my pleasant company," she said.

"And grand company it is!" As he poured himself another shot from the full bottle, he noticed me. His wide grin made his red beard stick out. "Ah, it's himself, here again, my boon drinking companion Dan O'Shamble!"

"I'm your zombie detective, not a drinking companion. You need your own UTI sponsor if you're going to go on a bender."

The leprechaun made a raspberry noise. "That cyclops is blind to everything I do for him! Though I have to say I miss the big guy."

"And I'm here to fix that," I said. He offered me a drink. I offered him the door. When he didn't get my hint, I grabbed him by the shamrock and pulled him off the stool.

When that wasn't good enough, I tweaked his ear and he let out a high-pitched yelp like a banshee. But I had met actual banshees before, and I was not intimidated. "I'm going to drag you to the cave, and I'm going to sit there while you two work it out."

"But it's no use!" he wailed.

"Believe me, Mr. O'Cream, I have spent more than my share of time on pointless endeavors."

The leprechaun kept struggling until I realized he was just

trying to reach for his whiskey bottle. Once I let him have it, it served as a kind of pacifier. As I hauled him out of the Goblin Tavern, Francine called out as she wiped down the far side of the bar. "Shamble, you know I love you, but who's going to pay his bar bill?"

"Sorry, Francine," I said, embarrassed. "Put it on McGoo's tab."

Though the leprechaun's legs were short, he hopped and skipped along, scuffing his black boots on the sidewalk. "Meself, I'd never underestimate a cyclops with an eyeball grudge, O'Shamble. The only way he'll forgive me is if you solve the case and decipher my note."

"I brought the note with me so we can all solve it together. And if that doesn't work, at least I'll make you bury the hatchet."

"Oh, don't ever give Ulysses a hatchet! He's blind— imagine what he might hit."

"We'll make do with a metaphor. Real hatchets are too dangerous."

At the cave subdivision, I knew I'd find the one-eyed brute (minus one eye) still moaning in the main living grotto. Nervous, Bailey hid behind me as if I could protect him from the wrath of Ulysses.

His former sponsor was sprawled on the cushionless sofa with his eye socket staring at the ceiling in a typical "depressed cyclops" pose. Right away, I noticed the distinctively clean air and the unexpected lack of marijuana smoke.

I tried to wake him gently. "Mr. Clops? I brought someone who wants to make amends. He says he's sorry."

Ulysses lurched into a sitting position, and the springs creaked. "Bailey's back?" He sounded delighted.

"And he's sorry," I said.

The leprechaun grimaced. "By my four-leaf clover, I never said I was sorry!"

"You're both sorry, or I'm going to make you both sorry." It was the best threat I could imagine. McGoo would have been proud of my tough-guy imitation.

"I'll have him back," the cyclops said, facing the wrong direction. "I'm sorry, too. I need my leprechaun sponsor so much."

Bailey simmered with indignation, but I could tell he was softening. "Well, no need to get my shillelagh in a knot...as long as Ulysses apologizes, too." He lowered his voice to a mutter. "I didn't mean to misplace your eyeball."

"I sure wish we could find it," Ulysses said.

I took out the note for handy reference, but the squiggles still made no sense.

The cyclops straightened. "Right now, though, can you to take me to the head shop? Please? You know the way. I'm starting to get really bad cravings. I need my special blend of pot—the Acapulco Gold you always get for me. Remember, you put in a special order with Consuela? It's got to be there by now."

"Yes, laddie, it should have arrived a few days ago, but I wasn't inclined to pick it up for you." He straightened his hat, still holding on to a bit of his pride.

"Wait a minute," I said. "Acapulco Gold? Pot?" I held out the Chinese menu with the leprechaun handwriting. "Does this say *gold* and *pot*?"

The leprechaun hopped into the air and clicked his heels together. "You've done it, O'Shamble! Why didn't I see it before? I wrote a reminder to retrieve the eyeball when I picked up his special order." He jabbed his small finger at the scribble. "That scrawl right there—it plainly says Acapulco next to gold. And pot. It's clear as day."

"It's not very clear to me," I said.

The leprechaun scratched his red beard. "I meant clear as a soft day in Dublin, where it's almost never clear."

The cyclops lurched up from the sofa. "Does that mean you remember where you've stored my eye?"

Bailey chuckled. "Sure and I do, every bit of it. I put that eyeball of yours in a neat little box and took it to the head shop. Since we're such frequent customers, Consuela was happy to put it in safekeeping for us." He sniffled. "Mind you, I just forgot what the note meant, that's all."

VIII

Consuela's dispensary was conveniently, and accurately, called Head Shop, and the proprietor was, also accurately, just a head.

Consuela had large brown eyes, full red lips, and long raven hair draped around the base of her neck—which was where she stopped. The head rested on an ornate silver platter with two burning novena candles behind her. Her expression lit up when we entered the shop, the leprechaun leading the blind cyclops. I closed the door behind us.

"Ai, my friend Ulysses! I thought you'd never come back."

"Grand to see you, Consuela," Bailey said. "Ulysses and meself, we've had some wee relationship difficulties."

"And also handwriting difficulties," I added. "Not to mention memory difficulties."

The head shop was a dim and crowded place. Racks of shelves held glass jars of dried buds labeled with clever or arcane names. Display shelves at the front counter held packaged and delicious-looking edibles, which were heavily regulated because unnatural species reacted differently to medicinals. I saw packages of dried leaves, dried flowers, and dried mushrooms, as well as mandrake root and exotic herbs. The labels suggested they were beneficial for any sort of health disorder suffered by any sort of creature, as well as the perfect ingredients for all witches' brews.

The cyclops blundered forward, knowing his way by instinct. He stopped in front of Consuela's head. "Do you have my order ready?"

I added, "More important, do you have his eyeball?"

Consuela turned her dark eyes toward Ulysses, which was the best she could do because she had no muscles to turn her entire head. "Both important questions, and the answer is yes to both. You are one of my very best cyclops customers, and I am honored you trusted me with such an important responsibility."

Ulysses swelled his bare chest with pride. The leprechaun danced another jig.

"Your order is packaged up in the back as always," Consuela continued. "And your eyeball is perfectly safe, just as I promised." Her expression flinched and her jaw clenched. Her eyes moved back and forth, and she seemed to be straining, then she sighed. "I'm afraid one of you will have to fetch it for me. I keep forgetting that I don't have any limbs."

"And it's still in the little box?" Bailey asked. "It's a family heirloom for holding curios. And eyeballs."

"It is right under the counter—beneath my vertebrae."

Since I'd been hired to solve the case, I wanted to be the one to end it. I stepped around the counter, searched behind Consuela's flowing dark tresses, and found a lower shelf. It held a dirty coffee mug, a cashbox, a small bottle of hand sanitizer—all of them dusty from lack of use—and a small wooden curio box with a carved four-leaf clover.

"Found it!" Holding the box in my palm, I lifted the lid. A bloodshot eye the size of a navel orange stared back at me. Normally, that would have been alarming, but right now it meant complete success.

Ulysses held out his hands, fumbling in the air. The leprechaun bounced up and down. "Here, let me help, laddie!" He reached into the curio box and snatched out the eyeball.

"Oww! Be careful," the cyclops said. "You poked me in the eye."

"Don't worry. I brought saline in my bag o' holding."

"Good thinking," I said.

Bailey handed the eyeball to Ulysses, who popped it firmly into the center of his forehead. "Ahhh!" He blinked furiously, then rolled his eye around and stared at me. This was the first time he'd actually gotten to look at his zombie private investigator. "I can see clearly now!"

The leprechaun returned from the back room, skipping along as he carried a package marked *Ulysses S. Clops*. The cyclops's eye widened with anticipation.

"Here you go, boyo, your Acapulco Gold. And I am glad to be your UTI sponsor again."

"I hope you'll be more careful next time," I said. "Or at least more legible."

"We will," Ulysses said.

"It'll be a real shindig!" the leprechaun said, and the two left arm in arm.

"They'll be back," Consuela said to me from her platter, still smiling. "I love repeat customers."

"That's a good business practice," I agreed, but I hoped I would not be seeing those two again.

WAITING FOR THE HUNGER
NINA KIRIKI HOFFMAN

Acclaimed veteran fantasy writer Nina Kiriki Hoffman allowed us to reprint one of the wildest and craziest stories ever written, "Savage Breasts," in Issue Zero of this magazine. In fact, it started off that very first issue.

Nina can not only write fantastically fun fantasy, but she can grab a reader and make them think. This is one of those great stories.

Nina is a musician, a writing instructor, and a judge for Writers of the Future. And amazingly fun to be around if you get the chance.

WAITING FOR THE HUNGER

NINA KIRIKI HOFFMAN

S alt soaks the air, even in this tightly closed little house. Through the shredding curtains I see the moon walking the waves, bleaching the beach they whisper on. I have insisted on light; she found and lit three candles. The air in the house is so still the flames never waver. Her plump face hovers above the flames, the rampant spills of her curls touched with gold. The yellow underlight makes a winged shadow-shape of her upper face--the shadow of her nose its spine, the shadows of her cheeks its wings, outspread, below her eyes.

"When was the last time you let yourself feel your hunger?" I ask. My voice sandpapers my throat on its way out. I try to shift my hands, but my wrists are bound too tightly together. I feel my feet swelling. I am convinced she has cut off the circulation in my ankles, though she insists she has had a lot of experience with ropes and with the traceries of veins and arteries; she says she never cuts off circulation.

In the midst of my discomfort, I regret that she tied me up

while I was deeply asleep. I missed feeling the touch of her fingers.

She looks down, the shadows sliding up her face. The reflections of flames in her eyes brighten. I tell myself they are only reflections; her eyes do not burn with interior fire. What she has told me about herself is only moon-spinning.

I have trouble believing my self-talk.

The house smells of mildew and wood rot, with a faint tang of marshland. No one has lived here for a long time.

Ruby touches her belly. It is globed and full as the moon. "Doctor, I feel hungry all the time," she says. "I've talked to others. They say it's not real hunger. But it gnaws at me. I try to resist." She rubs her temple, then glances up, the flames shining in her eyes. "Most of the others eat about every three days, and they don't need much. But once I start eating, I can't stop until it's too late. I hate myself." She twists her hands in her lap. "I hate what I do. Sometimes I want to kill myself, but I'm not strong enough."

"There are different kinds of hungers, Ruby," I say. My voice comes easily now that I am discoursing on my specialty, the treatment of eating disorders. "There are mental, emotional, and physical hungers. If you can listen to your hungers, you can learn to tell them apart. You can't feed an emotional or mental hunger with food. The more you try, the less you satisfy yourself." I blink, and realize that this is not my office in New Haven, and Ruby is not one of my regular patients.

"I'm hungry for something else?" She touches her mouth, which is slightly open. Her teeth are not ordinary. Her lips are generous, a deep color I suspect would be red in normal light.

"You could be hungering for love, attention, satisfaction.

You could be hungering for your true self, for all the things you needed and never received. Most of my patients eat when they're angry; they've never felt safe expressing anger, so they stuff it down with food. Anger is persistent; it takes a lot of food to keep it quiet."

Ruby rises and turns her back on me. Her full-length dress was once white; it is tattered and stained now, its hem muddied and stepped on. Through small rips in the fabric I catch glimpses of her body. It is smooth, pale, desirable. I remember why I decided to specialize in this field. I have always loved large women.

In college I deemed this perverse, so I studied how to cure their affliction, instead of working on my own. I majored in nutrition and psychology as well as general medicine. Now I live in a cauldron of uncertainties, as women I adore enter my office, learn what their fat is really trying to tell the world, learn to speak with their mouths as well as their bodies, and change into women I couldn't care less about.

Ruby is one of the beautiful ones, more lovely large than she would be thin. Her features have grace and clarity. I know this even though I have not seen her by daylight. Even under these circumstances--my wrists bound to each other and my ankles tied to this chair--I find myself falling in love with her.

"You think I'm angry?" she asks, turning back. For a moment she stands still, though I sense a lot of activity going on behind her face. Her hands tighten into fists. "I never get angry." Her voice shakes.

"Why not?"

"Anger destroys people. It reaches out and rips them to shreds." Her hands open. She stares down at her naked palms. "I watched what my father's anger did to me, and to the other kids. He twisted us all up. I got the younger ones away, most of the time, so he'd concentrate on me, but I'm never going to get mad like that and hurt people."

"You never got mad back?"

"Once, I did. Just once." She flexes her arm. "It never set quite right, but now it's okay," she says, looking at her forearm. "I thought maybe everything gets fixed, this side of the grave, but my appetite's still out of control."

"Your appetite isn't a physical thing; it's other things, turned sideways." I feel my curiosity rise, wanting to study how she has changed. But I can't think about that now. "How many children in your family?"

"Four."

"And you're the eldest? You tried to take care of them?"

"Tried to? I did take care of them. Somebody had to, with Mama gone since I was seven, and Papa--Papa...whenever they needed something, I figured some way to get it for them. I kept them clean. I bought them new shoes. I made their lunches and sent them off to school on time. We stuck together. I raised them good." She smiles, her eyes looking over my shoulder. "I wonder how they're doing now." She frowns. "I've been afraid to go back and check up on them. The hunger..."

Her arms go around herself. "I always took care of everything, Doctor. When this man, Darcy, started seeing my sister Linda, I tried to find out about him. Nobody knew where he came from or anything about him, so I told him to stop seeing her. After that, he came to see me. Papa couldn't stop him. Darcy told me he'd make me strong, like him. I thought if I was stronger I could deal with Papa and make the kids safe forever. But first I got sick..."

She paces away, stands with her face to the wall for a

moment, comes back. "Everything changed when I got sick. The kids got mad at me, and so did Papa. They all thought the roof caved in. 'Ruby's not supposed to get sick. Who's going to take care of the housework? Who's going to pay the bills if Ruby's not working? Who's going to phone in sick when Papa's been drinking too much?'"

"Who's taking care of Ruby while she's sick?" I ask. Her story is familiar to me in outline; I have heard it from many women. Every time, though, it hurts me. Every time my own response confuses me.

Of course, I never get sick either.

"Why, nobody really knew what to do for me. I'd never been sick before." She walks to the window, lays her hand flat on the glass a moment, then lifts it away. Living hands leave a print on cold glass. Ruby's hand leaves no mark. "I felt so tired, and I felt so evil for watching them run around wondering how to take care of themselves. Linda, she was always the wild one, but she tried to cook. She brought me a rose and all I could do was cry. I wanted to get better right away and get things back to normal, but I couldn't. Darcy came for me three times. He shared himself with me. He said he would give me power, and he did."

She turns toward me. Half her face is silvered by the moon, half burnished by candlelight. A tiny sob rises in her throat. "On the third day, I rose again, and I tried to go home to them. I wanted to make sure they were all right. I was walking home--I hadn't yet learned to fly--when the hunger rose in me, and I couldn't stop it. Three people died by the time I woke up. My hunger eats me up, and I can never escape it until too late." She looks at her hands. "It's been six years, Doctor. I can't go on this way. Most of the others like me survive on just a little blood--a couple mouthfuls--

they can stay in one place a long, long time without people noticing. I can never stay anywhere more than a week--people die and the police start looking for me. I can't stand doing this anymore."

She puts her hands to her cheeks. "When I found that copy of the *Gazette*, with the article about your work, I thought--can you help me?"

I look down at my hands. Though I am certain the circulation is cut off, my long fingers are pale, not purple with congested blood. My class ring is heavy on the third finger of my left hand. I have married my career, since I cannot find a woman I love without working to make her unlovable. I look up at Ruby. "You want me to help you stop bingeing? I don't think we can do that in one night."

Her hands grip each other. She closes her eyes a moment.

She smells like ripe apricots.

"Work like this takes years, Ruby."

"I don't have years." She stares at me, then comes back to sit facing me across the candles. She reaches out to touch a pulse point on my neck. "You don't either. Help me, Doctor. I feel the hunger waking, and you're the closest blood."

I hunch my shoulders, feeling exhaustion along the lines of my bones. I said goodbye to my last patient at five p.m., left my secretary to close up the office for the weekend, and drove two hours to come here to Greystone Bay. I have my retreat here, a converted apartment upstairs in one of the Victorian houses on North Hill; I spend my weekends here alone, walking the pebbly beach, into the fog and away from my work.

After I had some of "the best chowder on the coast" at the Golden Oyster, I went home to bed...and woke in this house from a sleep deeper than any I am accustomed to. I know where we are. Out the window, I can see Blind Point across the bay. We are in a deserted beach house north of town, between the sea and the marshes, one of a scattering of houses an ambitious developer built in the twenties, hoping to establish another Jazz Age getaway, but the lost generation did not want to get quite this lost; the project withered. I have walked past these rotting houses on windy days, when they seemed ready to blow away like paper. No one lived here for long, and no one lives here now.

No rescue will walk in off the midnight beach.

At first I thought Ruby was crazy, with her talk of blood. Now my doubts are gone.

"There are several steps to this," I say, letting my training take over. "The first thing you must do is accept yourself just the way you are. Until you love yourself, there is no hope for change."

"Doctor, haven't you heard me? How can I accept myself when I can't forgive myself? I am a hateful, evil creature. I am totally out of control. I break commandments to survive."

"Cast out everything you've been taught. Everything you know is wrong. Recognize you have always done the best you could with the information you had at the time. Say this: 'I, Ruby, love and forgive myself unconditionally.'"

Sobs shake her, but they make no noise and no tears. She tries to repeat the affirmation. She breaks down on the third word. She covers her face with her hands.

"Ruby, I love and forgive you unconditionally," I say. I feel this is true, but it hurts me to say it, because once she believes me, the balance will start to tip, and she will be her own person. She will reclaim the power she never knew she gave away. I sigh. "I love you, Ruby."

"How can you? I don't believe you! I'm awful, worse than Papa!"

"Ruby, I love you. I love you. No matter what you've been, no matter what you've done, no matter what's been done to you. I love you."

She rises and comes around the table, to stand between me and the light, a large dark silhouette. "You lie. No one could love me." She leans closer. I wonder if she sees better in the dark than I. Her clothes smell of rot, but her own scent is musk and apricots. I look up toward her eyes, knowing my love is naked in my face. "You love me," she whispers. Then, louder, "You must be crazy."

"Throw the beliefs away, Ruby, or we'll never get this done."

She gasps. "What?" she whispers.

"Throw away your beliefs. You are not evil. You are not horrible. You are a perfect being. Say it. 'I, Ruby, am perfect the way I am.'"

"I, Ruby..." She stumbles away, bumping the table. She staggers toward the wall and puts her face against it.

"Say it."

She says it, sarcastically. She turns to face me.

I smile at her. "You have to say it as though you believe it. We can't go any further until you convince me you believe it. 'I, Ruby, am perfect the way I am. I, Ruby, love and forgive myself unconditionally.' Say it. And feel it."

She speaks in the night, sometimes loudly, sometimes very softly. The moon rises above the house and out of sight, leaving light and shadows behind. Ruby alternates between fighting me and fighting everything she has ever learned. She paces. She screams at me. Once she stalks toward me and lays her hand against my throat, lifting her lip to show me her teeth. Her canines are longer than usual, but I forget to be afraid. The candles melt down to puddles of pleasant-smelling wax.

At last she stands in the center of the floor, her feet planted firmly, her hands on her hips. "I, Ruby, am perfect the way I am. I love myself unconditionally. I forgive myself--I forgive myself completely!"

At last I believe her.

"Listen," I say. My voice is hoarse. "I hear that you believe that now, but your resolution will falter. When that happens, there is a source of strength you can call on. Address it however you please. Some call it God. I think of it as my second self. When you need help, ask for it. It will come."

"I don't believe you! Are you a doctor or a priest?"

"I'm a midwife. You asked me to help you give birth to a new self, Ruby. I'm doing my job. This is one of the steps in the procedure. Believe in a force you can draw on for strength." My head falls forward. The excitement and challenge of the work no longer sustain me; I am too tired.

"Well, all right. If I can believe I'm a perfect being, I suppose I can believe in The Force." She sits on the floor at my feet. She touches my knee. The candles have dwindled to weak blue flames. "Doctor," she murmurs, "I'm hungry."

"Is it a physical hunger? Consult your body."

She sits a moment in silence, her head lowered. "Yes," she says at last.

"If it is a physical hunger, you should take care of it." The words are coming out of me by rote. "Think of what you most want to eat. Don't settle for anything else." I shake my head, trying to wake up. I cannot believe what I just said. "The secret now is to eat slowly. Pause often and ask yourself if you are satisfied. When you are satisfied, stop eating. Know there will always be food. You don't have to eat it all now. You can have more tomorrow, or whenever you want it."

She sits still a long moment, staring up at me. I glance out the window. False dawn lights the line between sea and sky.

Ruby rises to her feet. She comes to me, gently lifts my chin. Her lips are warm against my neck; her breath smells of ripe fruit. I close my eyes.

I wonder if I will be awake when she stops.

SCROOGE AND MARLEY

DAVID H. HENDRICKSON

Full-time professional writer David H. Hendrickson has been a writer for many, many years, not only as a fiction writer, but writing thousands of sports articles. He knows writing. And he knows life. In this story, Dave takes a look at the classic holiday story, only through the eyes of a hardboiled and washed-up detective.

Dave's short fiction has appeared in Best American Mystery Stories, Ellery Queen's Mystery Magazine, Heart's Kiss, *and numerous anthologies, including over a half dozen issues of* Fiction River *and just about every issue of* Pulphouse *so far. Check it all out at http://www.hendricksonwriter.com/*

SCROOGE AND MARLEY

DAVID H. HENDRICKSON

The midnight hour passed. I sat alone in my pitch-black office, surrounded by the smells of Jim Beam whiskey, cigarettes, and cheap perfume. The cheap perfume, imagined; the Jim Beam and cigarettes, real.

I took a drag on my cigarette, its glowing tip the only illumination in the tiny, boxlike room. I gulped down more whiskey. It burned all the way down, fed the fire in my gut. Outside, the shadows of the glowing streetlights shone on whores and thieves practicing their professions, identical but for the silence of thieves. I put my feet up on my desk and readied myself for another night of restless sleep.

She moved into my office looking like a luminescent angel, all soft curves, moist lips, and flowing chestnut-colored hair. Glowing but transparent at the same time. My kind of dame, except for the transparent part. I'd gotten my wish for perfume, though maybe not so cheap. Jasmine and honeysuckle. Not too strong, not too weak.

"You're here awfully late," she said, her voice as soft and silky as a pair of expensive stockings.

I didn't explain. She didn't need to know that I'd been kicked out of my apartment.

"So are you." I took my feet off the desk.

A grin formed at the corners of her mouth. It made her look even more beautiful. She batted her eyelashes. I hate when dames do that, mostly because I like it.

"You can hit the light switch over there," I said, pointing to the barren wall next to the door, now visible in her glow.

"Why bother?" she said. She had a point.

I took another drag from my cigarette. Blew the smoke off to the side. I gestured to the chair on the other side of my desk, the only other piece of furniture in the place. "Have a seat."

"I'm fine."

I stood so that I'd tower over her instead of the other way around, then felt silly as my legs wobbled and I had to steady myself with a palm flat on the desk.

"If you insist," she said. She smoothed her diaphanous gown and sat in the chair. Almost. She hovered above it a few inches, showing off, getting the upper hand back.

It was a nice trick but I wouldn't give her the satisfaction of a comment. I eased myself back into my chair, took a long drag from my cigarette.

"Could you put that out?" she asked.

"No."

But after another puff, I stubbed it out, its glowing embers disappearing in the overflowing ashtray.

"I can't pay you."

I crossed my arms, my rumpled suit bunching in the elbows, and leaned back. If I had a dime for every time I'd heard that line, I'd still have my apartment. I waited for the batting of eyelashes, the crossing of legs, the unspoken promise of making it worth my while.

I got none of them.

She stared at me coolly. "But I can make you famous. Maybe even immortal."

Famous caught my attention; *immortal* lost it. This dame was a looker, but I wasn't ready to die for her. I wished she'd just offered to make it worth my while even though the prettiest of them usually considered a peck on the cheek adequate payment for services rendered.

At least I knew how to turn that down. I didn't know how to turn down *immortal*.

"I'm listening."

"I'm looking for justice."

Of course she was. They all were. I readied myself for a tale of adultery, which was most of what my business involved, then reminded myself that this woman was mostly transparent. She wasn't like all the others. I'd gotten lost in her eyes and the silk-stockings voice.

Either that or it was the Jim Beam. I licked my lips, thirsty for another belt, but rested my hands in my lap.

"Go ahead," I said.

"He's gotten away with murder."

That caught my attention.

"He's a hero," she added. "I'm not looking to take all of that away from him, but people need to know the whole story."

I pulled a pad of paper close to me and grabbed a pen. The dim light of her glow would be barely enough to see.

"Who's the victim?" I asked.

"Jacob Marley."

I stared at her, not writing anything down.

She nodded. "Yes, that one."

"And you are?"

"Haven't you figured it out?"

I said nothing.

"At least narrowed it down?" she asked.

Still nothing.

"Well, you're no Sam Spade," she said.

That was a cheap shot, but I couldn't defend myself without looking weak. So I said nothing.

We waited each other out. Finally she spoke.

"I'm the ghost. The Ghost of Christmas Past. Call me Past for short."

I set the pen down on the desk. I wouldn't be needing it. I'd have to be dead myself if I couldn't remember this.

"Ann Rutherford played you in the movie," I said. "You're not real. Neither is Jacob Marley. You're make believe."

She looked about the room, then fixed me with her eyes. "More alive than you."

I kept my face as blank as I could but read a look of recognition in her eyes. She'd scored a bull's-eye and knew it.

I fumbled for another smoke and lighted it, silently cursing the trembling in my hand, slight but perceptible. I took a deep drag and blew the smoke toward her face.

I grasped the pad and pen. "And the murderer?"

"Ebenezer Scrooge."

———

ast, as I came to think of her, led me over to The Other Side, where all tales are true. Or at least true enough. We traveled through a fog so thick and wet I had to dry my face and eyes over and over again. The wind roared in my ears and whipped my hair all about.

After a dizzying time, the fog cleared and we came to an intersection where a busy marketplace extended north to south and east to west. People thronged about in all directions. Merchants called out, advertising their wares, in a language that sounded barely English, its accent so strong.

"Figs!" one cried. "Ripe apples just plucked from the trees!"

"Fresh chickens and a plump, juicy duck!" another called out.

"Thick coats of all types!" a third cried. "Guaranteed to keep you warm and shield you from disease!"

Past pulled me along. Snowflakes cascaded down, forming a carpet that crunched underfoot. The clomping of horses' hooves and the smell of manure filled the air.

"Where are we?" I asked, plumes of breath forming before my eyes.

She looked away, disappointed. Bells pealed from a towering white church on the corner.

"This is London?" I asked, knowing it to be so. "The London of Scrooge and Marley? Of Bob Cratchit and Tiny Tim? Of all you ghosts?"

"Aren't you the smart detective?" Past asked. "You put the clues together so well. You're worth every penny I'm paying you."

Another man might have slapped her. She had dragged me

to this world and now was toying with me as if I were but a mouse to her sly and devilish cat.

"Why me?" I asked. "If I'm nothing but a fool in your eyes?"

"And a drunken one at that."

I felt my cheeks grow warm despite the chill wind and the snowflakes, dropping one by one on my face.

"If you think to mock me—"

"I chose you because none better than you would listen to my plea."

"None better? What is that to mean?"

"I asked them all, starting, of course, with Sam Spade. I went right on down the line. They all declined. Until I came to you."

"Scraping the bottom of the barrel," I said bitterly.

"The lowest barrel of all," she said. Her voice sounded not at all like silk stockings anymore. It grated and rasped, no more feminine than a braying mule.

"If you couldn't persuade those *better than I*, perhaps the fault was your own. One of the other ghosts might have been more convincing."

Her face colored.

I smiled. For a change, *I* had scored a bull's-eye. I drank in her silence like a fine, aged bottle of Jim Beam.

"The other ghosts would not cooperate," she said after a time. "This mission is my own."

"Why won't the other ghosts cooperate? Why have Spade and all the others—*my betters*, as you put it—all turned you down?"

She thrust her shoulders back and her eyes blazed. "They don't want to hear the truth. The transformation of Ebenezer

Scrooge is too romantic a comfort to be taken away. It is too great a story. They prefer to believe a lie."

I considered her words for a time. "Why should I be any different?"

She blinked a snowflake from an eyelash and in that instant of distraction I saw compassion flicker ever so briefly in her eyes. "Because you have already lost, or freely given away, every last romantic ideal, every last comfort to the soul, you have ever held dear. You have nothing more to lose."

———

I needed a drink and a smoke. Past wouldn't hear of it. I'd never been one to let a dame order me around, but I'd never been around a dame like this one, one who had just transported me back a hundred years to mingle with people who don't really exist.

But here I was.

Across the street a man with a pointed nose poked his head out a window and called out to a boy below.

"What day is it today?" the man asked, his hair disheveled, his eyes red, and his lips blue.

"Eh?" asked the boy.

"What's today, my fine fellow?" the man asked.

"Today?" the boy replied. "Why, Christmas Day."

"It's Christmas Day!" the man said. I recognized him now as Ebenezer Scrooge. "I haven't missed it. The spirits have done it all in one night. They can do anything they like. Of course they can. Of course they can. Hello, my fine fellow!"

"Hello!" the boy said.

"Do you know the Poulterer's, in the next street but one, at the corner?" Scrooge asked.

"I should hope I did."

"An intelligent boy!" Scrooge said. "A remarkable boy! Do you know whether they've sold the prize turkey that was hanging up there. Not the little prize turkey. The big one?"

"The one as big as me?"

"What a delightful boy!" Scrooge said. "Yes, my buck."

"It's hanging there now."

"Is it?" Scrooge said. "Go and buy it."

The boy turned away.

"No, no," Scrooge said. "I am in earnest. Go and buy it, and tell them to bring it here, that I may give them the direction where to take it. Come back with the man, and I'll give you a shilling. Come back with him in less than five minutes and I'll give you half-a-crown."

The boy began to run away and all eyes in the square turned to Scrooge.

"Hey, kid," I called to the boy. He looked at me in startled wonder as if I were a pink elephant or a fish with legs. I waved him over.

"Who are you?" he said. He had bushy red hair and freckles all over his pudgy face. "I haven't ever seen you before."

"I'd like to talk to you about Mr. Scrooge."

"Is this a new scene?" He brightened. "Are they giving me a bigger part? I'd love a bigger part."

"No, I'd just like to talk to you."

His shoulders slumped. "I knew it. I'll never get a bigger part." He shrugged. "I shouldn't complain, I guess. We *are* immortal."

The word stopped me in my tracks for an instant before I recovered. "Tell me about Scrooge."

"What about him?"

"How long have you known him?"

The kid looked confused. "For the entire story, of course. What kind of question is that?" He cocked his head. "Who are you?"

He glanced at Past and dawning recognition swept over his face. "You're with her, aren't you? You're not even in the story."

"No, I'm not in the story. I just want to—"

"You want to ruin Mr. Scrooge. Just like her." He pointed to Past.

"I just want to find out the truth."

"Who cares about the truth?" the kid said. "It doesn't matter. The story is brilliant. People will always remember it. They'll remember us. They'll remember me. It's a small part, but they'll remember me. My big grin." He smiled broadly. "My happiness when Mr. Scrooge orders the huge turkey. 'The one as big as me?' I say. 'It's hanging there now.'"

"Yes, yes," I said, dismissively waving my hand. "I've heard it."

All subtlety was wasted on this boy, so I went right to the heart of the matter.

"Do you think Ebenezer Scrooge killed Jacob Marley?"

The kid's smile disappeared. His face contorted in hatred. He spat on my shoes. "Do you really think I'll let you take down Mr. Scrooge? So what if he killed Marley? Maybe Jacob Marley deserved to die. I don't know. I don't care. It *doesn't matter.*"

"It doesn't matter if—"

"If you take down Mr. Scrooge, you take down us all," the kid said. "You'll deny all the future generations the pleasure of his story. Redemption. A new man. All that twaddle. And for what? The truth? Who cares?"

The kid pointed to Past. "She's the only one who cares. She's crazy! She's got immortality—and *a big part!*—but she's trying to throw it away." He turned to face her. "You can be replaced, you know."

"It's the truth and you know it," Past said. "Everyone does."

"You ruin Mr. Scrooge," the kid said, "and all of us...we'll just go away. Disappear." He looked just a little bit haunted. "Now leave me be."

He turned to run away, then glanced over his shoulder in my direction, looking just a little bit fearful. "You can't have my role. It doesn't suit you at all, you know. You're far too old. It needs to be a boy."

And with that, he was off.

———

Word got around fast. No one else would talk to me, so I watched the performances play out, over and over, and pieced it together myself.

Past was right. Scrooge had murdered Marley for greed, pure and simple. Why share profits with a partner when you can have it all? I watched closely that briefest of flashbacks which showed Scrooge conducting a great deal of business in the wake of Marley's death. *He was an excellent man of business on the very day of the funeral*, Dickens wrote.

Marley never suspected, not even after death. I might have

thought from his position in hell, the devil might have tormented him further. Let him know of his partner's treachery. But maybe even the devil has his bounds. Not even he could be allowed to puncture the myth of Ebenezer Scrooge's redemption.

In truth, I needed no more confirmation than the fear in every man and woman's eyes. They saw me as their own personal Grim Reaper. When I took down Scrooge, I would at the same time end their lives, their immortality.

Not one would talk to me. Not with Past by my side. Not with her off playing her role, ready to rush back to me at the end of the first act.

I watched the performances in what amounted to the greatest of front row seats, enjoying them more and more each time, even becoming a part of the bustling crowds. Not at all like the old days when the very thought of Tiny Tim saying, "God bless us, every one," sent me grasping for my bottle of Jim Beam.

I felt a joy in the story I'd never experienced back in my old world. The general public would surely turn on Scrooge the Murderer. The newspaper columnists and clergymen would rail about a society rotten to the core and use Scrooge as their Exhibit A. As if that rotten core was news. As if they needed a torn-down Scrooge to make their point.

But for someone like me who had killed more than just once, Scrooge's redemption became all the more powerful. His hypocrisy in remaining silent—*"Oh Jacob Marley! Heaven, and the Christmas Time be praised for this!"*—bothered me not one bit. I had, after all, failed to confess any of my own crimes back in the old world.

So I considered it a special privilege to be given a personal audience with the great man himself. We spoke for hours, though it felt like seconds.

"What did he say?" Past asked, breathless, her voice urgent, when I emerged from the great man's house. The flush of excitement filled her face. "Did he confess?"

I tried to suppress my smile but could not. "Our conversation will remain private. I'll divulge not a word."

Her face fell. "Surely you jest."

My smile broadened.

She grabbed my arm. "Do not tease me on this matter."

"I tease you not."

"I should have let you rot in your whiskey," she said before stomping off, her hands shaking with rage.

Perhaps she should have.

———

After several more performances, Past came to me, but I silenced her until Tiny Tim said, "God bless us, every one."

Smiling, I turned my attention back to her. "Yes?"

"You must return to your people now and expose Scrooge for what he is. No mere miser who learned the spirit of Christmas, but a murderer of his best friend and a hypocrite."

"That he is," I said.

"So come with me. You will become famous even as Ebenezer Scrooge becomes infamous."

I didn't move.

"I am the Ghost of Christmas Past," I said.

The smile on her face froze. "What did you say?"

A sense of contentment, of purpose, came over me. I felt a glow inside that in my old life only Jim Beam gave me.

"These are but shadows of the things that have been," I said.

Her eyes widened.

I stepped toward her. "I've learned my lines."

She backed away.

But not fast enough.

WHEN THE COWS COME HOME

KEITH WEST

This was Keith West's first story in Pulphouse Fiction Magazine. *He takes the old saying that is his title and then gently moves us all to a head-shakingly different story.*

A total whacked-out Pulphouse-style story. Enjoy.

WHEN THE COWS COME HOME

KEITH WEST

Richard Drake sat in the rocking chair on his front porch, smoking his pipe and watching the sun set over the hill on the far side of the empty pasture. Aside from a mosquito that kept wanting to buzz in his left ear, he was enjoying a pleasant evening.

It had been a warm day and would have been hot had it not been for the breeze out of the north. He'd spent the afternoon repairing the fence on the south edge of his farm. A dozen of the wooden fence posts had rotted in the ground. They had been there since he was a boy, over forty years. He had gradually been replacing the old post oak fencing with metal posts.

Post oaks were the dominant tree in this part of Texas. They tended to grow straight, at least when they were young, and the early settlers had cut them down before they got too tall and used them for fencing. Hence the name, post oak.

It had been hard work, digging out the rotted wood and driving the metal posts into the ground by hitting them with a pipe closed at one end. The pipe had handles which he pulled down on to hit the post with the closed end of the pipe and drive it into the ground. Then he'd had to string the barbed wire. Richard knew he would be sore tomorrow, but at least he hadn't gotten any blisters this time. It would be a good sore, the best kind, the kind earned by hard and productive work.

But that would be in the morning, after he'd stiffened up while sleeping. Right now, he wanted to sit and rest and smoke his pipe.

For once he didn't mind that his wife Carol insisted he smoke outside. The evening was pleasant. The temperature was comfortable, the sunset a brilliant orange turning to red on the horizon. His belly was full of meat loaf, mashed potatoes and green beans grown in the garden out back, sweet tea, and peach cobbler.

Life was good.

Well, except for that pesky mosquito that kept buzzing in his ear.

Richard slapped at it, but all he succeeded in doing was to swat himself on the ear. The mosquito was back within seconds.

Richard sighed, exhaling a cloud of smoke. A gust blew the smoke back in his face. At first, he was annoyed that the wind had shifted direction. Then he realized that the smoke had also driven away the mosquito.

He turned his head so that when he exhaled, the smoke would blow to his left.

That seemed to solve the problem of the mosquito.

Now, he could enjoy the sunset and listen for the crickets to start chirping. He'd go to bed soon after that. The sound of the crickets would lull him to sleep almost as soon as his head hit the pillow.

He gazed out over the empty pasture, the grass grown high and starting to yellow in the early summer heat.

Richard rubbed his fingers across his chin. The stubble made a rasping sound as it scraped against his calloused hand. The empty pasture was the only thing that could ruin his contentment this evening.

There were no cows in the pasture.

One day last week, they'd simply vanished. And not just on his place. The Hendersons, the Garcias, and the Holcombs had all discovered their livestock was missing. Even the cattle at the Twisted Tee Ranch, which was owned by a large conglomerate now, had disappeared.

By the middle of the morning, all the news channels were covering the story. Every cow and bull of every variety, whether dairy or beef, had disappeared. Not just locally, but all over the world. No carcasses had been found anywhere, so the world hoped they were still alive somewhere.

India declared a national emergency. Masai tribesmen were wandering the veldt aimlessly. Rodeo clowns were out of work. McDonald's and Burger King were on the edge of bankruptcy. The internet was full of conspiracy theories involving UFOs, government cover-ups, and the Bermuda Triangle.

Richard was glad that cattle were only a small part of his operation. The bulk of his land was used for farming, mostly cotton with some wheat and a little corn. The cattle were mostly to provide milk, steaks, and hamburger for him and Carol, plus a few friends.

They'd survive financially, whereas the Holcombs probably wouldn't.

Still, seeing the empty pasture created an emptiness in his heart. Carol had liked to listen to their lowing. She said she found it soothing. He hurt just as much for her as he did for himself.

As the sun disappeared behind the hill and twilight began to turn to darkness, Richard knocked his pipe against the ashtray on the stand to the right of his rocking chair.

Time to get ready for bed.

He groaned as he stood up. His muscles had stiffened while he sat, and Richard had to push himself erect. Normally, he could stand without having to use his hands.

That was when the flash of light blinded his dark-adapted eyes.

At first he thought someone in a large vehicle had turned into the driveway with their high beams on. As he blinked, he realized that couldn't be right. The light was green, not white. He didn't know of any vehicles that used green light.

Could it have been a meteor? He hadn't seen any streak across the sky that a shooting star would leave to mark its passage. And there'd been no sound of an impact or shock wave from an explosion.

Richard rubbed his eyes.

Why wasn't his vision returning to normal?

He blinked some more, and the light coming through the screen door from the living room became visible. He looked in the direction the flash had come from.

Nothing.

He waited, and gradually the horizon became visible as a dark line below the stars. That was one advantage to living in the country. You could see the stars at night. There was nothing unusual. The driveway rounded a grove of mesquite trees which extended for nearly one hundred yards to the gravel county road.

Come to think of it, if a vehicle had been approaching his place, he should have heard it coming. Cars on gravel roads made noise.

That was when he heard the sound.

At first he didn't recognize it because it was so faint.

Then he realized it was a bell. A cowbell.

"Blossom?"

He whispered the name of Carol's favorite cow, the one she had bottle raised and wouldn't let him butcher. Instead, she provided them with fresh milk. Blossom was in many ways a part of the family. She was the only cow that wore a bell. Richard whispered the name, afraid if he said it out loud the sound of the bell would go away.

A cow lowed in reply.

"Blossom."

This time Richard said it as a statement of fact, not a question.

Richard moved toward the driveway. He nearly stumbled going down the steps and into the yard. If he hadn't grabbed the handrail along the steps, he would have fallen. As it was, he dropped his pipe.

He could find it later. Right now he had to see for himself that the cows had returned.

Dark figures rounded the grove of mesquites. They were bovine in shape.

One, two, three…

The cattle continued to walk around the mesquites and into the yard. The bell rang softly with each step Blossom took. Richard counted each one. Many he recognized by their silhouettes. There were fourteen in all, including the five calves that had been born earlier in the spring.

Blossom was in the lead. The white patch on her face was clearly visible in the starlight. The patch consisted of five ovals, their narrow ends all oriented toward their center. Carol had thought the pattern resembled a flower and had named the calf Blossom when she had been born.

"Carol," Richard called. Then louder, "Carol!"

Her reply came faintly through the screen door.

"What is it? What's wrong?"

"It's Blossom. She's come home. All the cows are home."

Carol burst through the screen door. She'd been wiping her hands on a dish towel, and as she left the house, she threw the towel onto the porch.

Carol's brown hair, streaked with gray which reflected the light from inside the house, was tied in a ponytail. The ponytail was almost horizontal as she came out of the house.

Carol had put on a few pounds since she and Richard had married, but you couldn't tell it by the way she flew down the steps. Where Richard had stumbled and almost fallen, Carol hardly touched them. Or so it seemed to her husband.

She threw her arms around Blossom.

"Oh, Blossom, where have you been? We've been worried sick about you."

"I'm fine, Carol. We went home for a meeting. I didn't want to alarm you, but it was urgent."

The cow spoke with a rich, low alto voice.

Carol gasped and fell backward onto her rump in shock. Richard started to try and catch her, but he was too late. She had already hit the ground before he started moving.

Carol scrambled backward like a crab.

"Richard, did Blossom just speak to me?"

"Yes," he said. He swallowed, his mouth dry.

"Don't be alarmed, Carol, Richard. I'm still your faithful cow. Always have been, always will be."

Carol had reached Richard, and she began to pull herself to her feet by grabbing onto Richard's jeans. He bent over to help her up. When she was standing, they wrapped their arms around each other.

"Am I going crazy?" she whispered.

"If you are, I'm going there with you."

"No," said Blossom. "You aren't going crazy. And you aren't hallucinating or imagining things. I'm really talking to you."

"Can the other cows speak?" asked Richard.

"Some can. Most have chosen not to. The procedure that allows me to talk is temporary. It's also uncomfortable, which is why most cattle don't take it. I felt you deserved an explanation."

"An explanation of what?" asked Carol.

"Where we've been. Although there's a lot I can't tell you. Some of it you wouldn't understand. Other parts are, well, I guess you could say they're secrets."

Behind Blossom, one of the cows dropped some patties in the driveway. The smell was rich and thick and carried on the breeze. Richard thought it had been one of the calves but he wasn't sure.

"Were," began Richard. He swallowed again. His mouth was dry, not just from his pipe but from what he was experiencing. Part of him thought he had to be dreaming. But the smell of the fresh patties, the feel of Carol's arms around his chest, and the sound of Blossom's voice convinced him he wasn't. He'd never had a dream so real.

"Were you kidnapped by aliens?" he managed to ask.

Blossom mooed. So did most of the other cows. Somehow Richard knew they were laughing at the question.

"No, we weren't," said Blossom, "but you're not that far off. Aliens were involved, but they didn't kidnap us."

Blossom chewed her cud for a moment before continuing.

Richard wanted to ask just what she meant, but he didn't know how to ask the question.

"There are aliens, several different groups of them. We work for one of them. Our job is to simply observe. Lately the taste of grass has been changing."

"Grass has a taste?" asked Carol.

"Of course it does. Different species of grass have different flavors, just like different fruits do to you."

"Like how apples have a different taste and texture than oranges do," said Richard.

"Exactly. Clover tastes different from alfalfa, and fresh grass tastes different than dried grass of the same variety."

"So, what does the taste of grass have to do with aliens?" Carol wanted to know.

"Everything as it turns out. If it had just been a local change, then the most likely cause would be something in the surrounding environment. But this was worldwide."

"Wait a sec," said Richard. "are you telling me that you can communicate with cows all over the earth?"

Blossom blinked.

"Yes, I am. We have ways of communicating that you don't."

"You mean like telepathy?" asked Carol.

"Something like that, although it isn't true telepathy as you probably mean. Let's just say we can communicate and let it go at that. I don't really know how to explain it, and I'm not sure I have the time if I did. As I told you, the procedure that lets me talk is uncomfortable and temporary."

Neither human said anything in reply.

"Once we started to realize that the strange taste was everywhere, although not all cattle thought the new tastes were the same everywhere, we knew something weird was going on. So we contacted the aliens who are in charge of protecting this planet."

"There are aliens watching over us?" asked Richard.

"After a fashion, although it's not just humans. It's the whole solar system, including the other life."

"Other life?"

"Earth isn't the only place in this solar system where life exists, Carol. Now, please, let me continue. My time is running short."

Carol nodded, her ponytail bouncing to the motion. Richard nodded once.

"The aliens who we work for, well, they resemble cattle in a general way. They have horns and tails and they are also ruminants. A few of us were selected for testing. I wasn't one of them, in case you were wondering.

"What they found was really alarming. They had noticed a rise in activity from a different alien race they were monitoring, but our aliens hadn't been able to figure out what the other aliens were up to. They suspected no good, but they didn't have any proof. Until they did, they couldn't act."

Another calf dropped a patty. Several of the younger cows

were beginning to shuffle their feet. Richard wasn't sure if it was nerves or if they were growing bored.

Blossom seemed unaware of the restlessness of her herd.

"Once they were able to do some tests, our aliens became quite alarmed and summoned all of us to one of their bases. It was a big base. It had to be to hold all of us."

"What was the problem?" asked Richard. "Why would they need to do that?"

"Because the change in the taste of grasses, and it wasn't all grasses, mind you, only some, was due to the interference of the other aliens."

"Do these aliens have names?" asked Carol.

"I can't pronounce them, and neither could you."

"It's all right, Carol," said Richard. "I'm following. Please continue, Blossom."

"Thank you, Richard.

"The other aliens, the ones up to no good, had introduced a slight change in the molecular structure of these specific grasses. And no, I don't know what all grasses were affected. But the ones that were affected were designed to create a change in milk. We cows wouldn't be affected by the change, but humans would. It would cause sterility in humans."

"Why?" asked Carol.

"So that your species would die off. Then this planet would be eligible for colonization."

"But you would still be here," she said, her voice and face full of horror.

Richard felt a slow burn of anger rising in his chest.

"It's not that simple. Interstellar law is quite complicated. To simplify, a planet can be colonized if there are no species using advanced technology. That is the basic standard."

"So are we safe?" asked Richard.

Blossom bobbed her head.

"Yes. That was why we all disappeared. Our aliens, the ones friendly to this solar system found a way to neutralize the changes the other aliens made. But the neutralization required all of the cows to undergo the treatment in person."

Two of the herd mooed in agreement. At least it seemed to Richard that they were agreeing.

"What about other animals, like sheep and goats? Weren't they affected?"

"No, this change would only affect cattle. Other animals were immune."

Richard stroked his chin, thinking. The stubble rasped against his hand.

"It sounds like," he said slowly, choosing each word carefully, "that you're talking about changes in DNA."

Blossom blinked.

"Yes, I think so. I don't know that term, but if you are talking about genetics in some form, your assertion would be correct."

"So everything is okay, now?" asked Carol.

Blossom had been looking at Richard, but now she turned her face to Carol.

"For the time being, at least." The other aliens, the ones causing all the trouble, will probably try something again, although not in my lifetime or even yours. But they've been wanting to move into this region of the galaxy for some time now. They don't give up easily."

"So what happens now?" asked Richard.

"I'd really like for you to open the barn. All this talking is not only hurting my throat, it's making me very thirsty."

Blossom swished her tail.

"Oh, of course," said Richard.

He disengaged himself from Carol's arms. Ever since the cows had disappeared, he'd locked the paddock and their barn. He headed to open it.

The cows followed. All but Blossom.

She walked up to Carol and nuzzled her. Carol wrapped her arms around Blossom's neck.

"Thank you, Blossom, for all you did. And welcome home."

"It's good to be home, Carol."

Blossom's voice was changing, sounding more like a cow lowing and less like human speech. The procedure that had allowed her to talk, whatever it had been, was wearing off.

Carol planted a big kiss right in the middle of the white pattern on Blossom's forehead.

Blossom turned and followed the rest of the cows. Richard had the barn door open and the lights turned on. When Blossom reached him, he also gave her a big hug. He refrained from kissing her, though.

After the cows were settled in, Richard and Carol sat in their rocking chairs on the front porch. The breeze was soft and pleasantly cool. The crickets were singing, but tonight Richard and Carol didn't pay any attention to the crickets. They held hands as they rocked and listened to the gentle lowing of their cows.

It was good to finally have them home.

THE SPIRIT HOUSE
LISA SILVERTHORNE

Acclaimed veteran fantasy and science fiction writer Lisa Silverthorne makes a setting come alive in this story like no other writer can. Amazing.

Lisa sells her fantastic short fiction to many, many markets, including a couple stories to the Holiday Spectacular. For a lot more about Lisa's stories and her growing new Game of Lost Souls series, and other new fantasy series, go to http://www.lisasilverthorne.com

THE SPIRIT HOUSE

LISA SILVERTHORNE

Cast your soul to the sea, he said to me once. From some stupid love poem he wrote. Donny always talks weird, in romantic images that are pretty but empty. Like Donny. He's serving ten to life down in Walla Walla. Sometimes I even miss him.

From this pier, if I close my eyes, I can still see him in those heavy boots walking the surf-soaked rocks where we used to sit and talk. He loves to walk the shore. Maybe that's why he says those stupid things? Maybe they somehow make up for the bad things he did—we did. I try to remember that, but sometimes, my head's all confused. It's the new rehab treatment they gave me today.

Carmen Slater, my probation officer, stands at the opposite end of the pier, waiting for me. She doesn't usually follow me around like this, but my community service starts today, so she's sticking close. I glance down at the thick black band around my ankle. This tracking device will lead them right to me if I decide to bolt. Not many places for a convicted felon to run.

Still, I'm lucky. I got out in five with a stint in rehab and community service. It'll be a year before I'm through with both. I didn't kill that guy in the alley that night (Donny did), but I did gank his money. Donny told the guy if he handed over his cash, he wouldn't shoot him. Stupid fool made Donny kill him. Over twenty bucks and a lousy credit card.

"Kip, it's time to go!"

I turn away from the ocean and stare blankly at Carmen with her severe black hair, stuffy lace blouse, and over-pressed blue skirt. Like some store window mannequin. Carmen taps her watch. "I need to get you to the hospice now." Her words are loud and slow. Don't know if she thinks I'm deaf or stupid. She reminds me of my fourth-grade teacher, always talking to me like I don't understand English. I hated Mrs. Williams. I don't have much use for Carmen either.

She motions me away from the pier and slowly, I comply. I'll come in my own time. Finally, I reach her and with a smirk, I slip past her into the car. I lean my face against the window to catch another glimpse of the ocean. My hair smells salty and clean from the breeze. Carmen frowns, but she puts on that fake, everything's-okay smile and slides into the driver's seat. Then she drives away, toward some stupid hospice where I'm supposed to do my CS. There's some experiment going on there and I'm part of it. Some choice—the rest of my prison term or some bullshit experiment. I'd rather be picking up trash in parks, but I guess my gig's easier than Donny's. He may never see the ocean again.

Carmen drives out of the parking lot and onto the highway. The Puget Sound flickers at the edges of the rocky, tree-covered shoreline rushing ahead of us. The pines are so tall and green against the bare trees around them. Autumn came fast this year.

My head still hurts from the rehab session. I thought it'd be some sort of therapy where they'd talk at me and give me drugs, but it turned into minor surgery. Some chaff about a device to signal some brain chemicals to be released. The doctor showed it to me. It's smaller than an aspirin. How can something that small do anything? I don't quite understand it all and I don't want this thing in my head, but it beats that rat-trap cell and getting a shiv in the gut some night. They say I don't know right from wrong, but this thing in my head does and eventually, it will teach me. One of the doctors calls it an artificial conscience. Guess if Donny and me had had this thing, he wouldn't have killed that jerk in Seattle. A twinge of pain ripples through my stomach and my hands start to shake, like I'm hungry or something.

"We're not far from the hospice, Kip," Carmen chirps from the front seat, all smiles and bouncy. Like we're going on a picnic. She's so fake she makes me sick. "It's just past Coupeville."

The blue and green water is bright against the steep cliffs that rise around us. I close my eyes, not realizing I've fallen asleep until Carmen gently nudges my shoulder.

"Kip, we're here. Kip?"

I step out of the car and stare at the cedar building on the hillside. With all its windows, it looks fragile, like a strong wind would knock it over. A thin curl of smoke rises into the gray sky. The air smells burnt.

"This is Crossroads Hospice," says Carmen. She carries my

duffle bag with her toward the front door and I have no choice but to follow. I hate this thing on my ankle.

A silver-haired woman opens the door and greets Carmen like a long-lost relative. She's short and squat and looks like she should have eleven grandchildren.

"Carmen, how are you? It's been ages, child!" The old woman hugs her.

"How are you, Miss Miller? It's so good to see you again." Carmen grips the old woman's plump arms.

The woman shakes a finger at Carmen. "It's Mary Margaret."

Carmen slips over to me and puts her hands on my shoulders, but I pull away. "Mary Margaret, this is Kelly Thorpe."

I sneer. I haven't been Kelly Thorpe in a long, long time. "I go by Kip."

The old woman's expression turns serious as she stares at me, looking through me. Uncomfortable, I look away. "You've got quite a bit of work ahead of you, Kelly Thorpe." She pauses and the hint of a smile touches her wrinkled, pale face. "Kip."

I shrug. So, I empty a few bedpans and change a few sheets. Big deal. Doesn't mean anything. In a year, I'll be out of here. I'll head south, toward San Diego. That'll be far enough from this state.

My stomach hurts again, but I keep a straight face.

Old Mary Margaret opens the door and waves me inside. I glare at her as I pick up my bag and walk past. She's gotta get the message right off that I'm not interested in being her friend. I'm just here to do my time. I'll be their little maze jockey as long as I get my chocolate bar.

The inside of this place looks like something out of those old, liver-colored photographs, where the clothes were bulky and fussy, full of lace and velvet and frills. Lots of fancy curtains and table coverings. Flowers everywhere. And it stinks of roses. I remember Donny taking me to a flower shop once. The case was full of roses, all kinds of colors, all kinds of smells. But this place reeks of them. Glass lamps sit in front of the windows and reflect light in little rainbows around the one big room. There are couches everywhere and eight or nine people sitting there in robes. Most of them stare blankly around the room through sunken eyes and hollowed faces. I smile. Like those store window dummies. Better them than me.

Old Mary Margaret's face tightens when she sees my smile. "Is there something you find amusing here, Kip?"

"This place looks more like a wax museum than a nursing home," I answer. Again, my stomach burns, the pain a little worse than before. I must be coming down with something.

Mary Margaret glares at me and points to the hallway. Smirking, I move toward it.

She walks ahead, past what looks like a dining room and kitchen. At the end of the hall is a large bunk room. There's thick pink and blue comforters on each bed. A blonde woman in blue scrubs walks through the room, adjusting covers, filling water pitchers that set on little, marble-top tables beside the beds. Most of the beds are filled with thin people, like they're going to kick off any minute.

"This where you keep the stiffs?" I ask.

Mary Margaret turns and grabs me by the shoulders. She shakes me hard, like I'd just spit on her shoes or something. Her face is all red and her lips are pressed together. I shove her away.

"Don't do that again," I say. I don't like people touching me.

A sharp pain rips through my gut and I cry out, falling to my knees. Her hands grip my shoulders again, but she doesn't shake me this time.

"Kip—"

I slap her hands away. "Leave me alone!"

Again, the pain rips through my gut like a knife blade and holds on. And I suddenly realize why. I should have felt guilt, but I didn't.

"I—I'm sorry," I mutter through clenched teeth. Only then does the pain let up.

A smile hints at the corners of Mary Margaret's wrinkled mouth.

"Are you all right?"

I nod. I am.

"All right," says Mary Margaret. She steps back, allowing me space to get up. I glance around the sick room, noticing the gray faces staring at me like I'm some freak.

"What are you all staring at?" I shout.

When they finally look away, I glare at Mary Margaret. Her smile has disappeared.

"Do you know where you are?" she says.

I shrug. Like I care.

"This is a *hospice*, Kip. A place where people come to die." She sighs and her face doesn't look so angry now. She motions toward a bed the woman in scrubs is straightening. "Mrs. Brandt passed early this morning and we were here to help her through it. I'll put up with your sneers and your irreverence everywhere but in this room. One word from me to Carmen Slater and you'll be back in prison, Kip—artificial conscience or not. Is that clear?"

I'm not sure what she means by irreverence, but I nod.

"All right then. I think you've seen enough for the day. I'll show you to your room and let you get settled. We'll start over tomorrow when you've gotten a little of the vinegar out of your system."

———

It feels weird having so much room to myself. I'm not used to spending the night in such a frilly, big room. The four-poster bed with its lace bows, all pink and sugary-sweet. It's enough to make me puke. I crawl out of the bed, my tracking anklet bulky and heavy as I stumble into the bathroom. If they can put this thing in my head to teach me how to act, why can't they do the same thing with this lousy anklet? Maybe it's because they don't want me to forget why I'm here and what I've done?

I scowl at the mirror. My mousy hair needs washing. I look at how much thinner I am than I was five years ago when they carted me off to prison. I'm not sure I know the person staring back at me, but I'm not sure I knew her any better five years ago.

After I stand around in the shower for a while, not having to watch my back for once, I towel dry my hair, dress, and wander into the hallway. I eventually find my way back to the foyer where Mary Margaret stands, looking tense.

"I was afraid you'd drowned down there."

"Hey, that's the first real shower I've seen in years. Give me a break."

Mary Margaret turns away and in a tired voice, she tells me to come with her. Time to run the maze. I follow. Where else am I going to go?

Down the hall again and we're in that huge bunkroom with its marble tabletops and comforters and sick people. The smell of old piss and bleach gags me. Old Mary Margaret whirls and shakes a finger at me.

"You remember what I told you yesterday, Kip. You'll show respect in this room."

I nod slowly. A lot of them are just old people past their time. I walk down the aisle, trying to pretend they aren't here with their wheezing and moaning.

I say, "It's kinda funny, don't you think? I helped Donny kill a guy and now, my community service is to help people die. I wasn't trying to be irrelevant or whatever."

Mary Margaret laughs. "Irreverent, Kip. Not irrelevant."

"Whatever," I say. "So how do I figure into this experiment?" I have to ask someone and Mary Margaret seems like she tells it straight. Not like Carmen. She just tells me what I want to hear.

"They want to test your implant in this environment. See if it gives you compassion."

"That's it?" I ask. How lame.

"No," she answers, her voice tired. "Kip, do you believe in the soul?"

I shrug.

"No one has proven it one way or another," she says. Her eyes seem to light up now, like she's really into this stuff. "Some University of Washington researchers are trying to answer that question. They're trying to measure the existence of the soul."

I smile. "I'd make a good test case. The judge said I didn't have one."

Mary Margaret laughs again. "They're only studying terminally ill patients, Kip." She points at two women in white scrubs standing at the end of a bed. The red-haired one's messing with a box on a table and the dark-haired one is typing stuff on a datapad. "They're measuring brain chemicals before and after death."

"Yeah, right. And whose dumb-assed idea was that?"

She straightens her back and I can tell I've made her mad again.

"It was mine."

I let the words settle for a moment. Not sure what I should say, but a pain in my stomach reminds me that maybe I've hurt her feelings.

"Sorry," I mutter. Just feels right somehow to say that. "Why'd you want to do this?"

"I'm getting old," she says with a sigh. Her voice is quieter now. The anger's going away. "I'd like to know where we go from here."

I've thought about that some, when the prosecutor asked for the death penalty for Donny. I don't know what's out there. Donny says there's nothing, just emptiness, but it makes me wonder sometimes. Especially when I look at the night sky and the ocean. Just feels like there should be more to it. Maybe that's why Donny likes to walk on the beach and stand at the edge of the water? Because, for a little while, it lets him wonder.

"You think there's something beyond here?" I ask, trying my best not to sound bitchy.

She smiles. "Yes, there has to be. Look at the mountains and the forests. There's order and reason to it, and we place our trust in that."

So many times I've wanted to believe things weren't just all out of control and everything. Like that night in the alley. It seems to hang in my thoughts more and more now.

"Your first assignment is to fill all the pitchers with water. When you're finished with that, there's laundry to fold and beds to make."

I do what she asks. I fill all the pitchers. Takes me a half hour, but I manage. When I'm finished, I find her sitting with a white-haired woman, whose face is all wrinkled and pasty.

"I'm done with the pitchers," I say. "Do you want me to start on the laundry?"

"Sit," she says, like I'm her dog.

"Why should I?"

"Because I asked you. Please."

I don't feel like arguing, so I sit.

"Kip, this is Mrs. Sanderson. She's eighty-three."

I stare blankly into the woman's pale green eyes.

"Hello, Kip," she says in a raspy voice. She smiles. "Thank you for sitting with me a bit."

I frown. Like it's my idea.

Old Mary Margaret nudges me with her shoe. Damn, she's expecting me to actually talk to this woman. "Uh, sure."

"You remind me of my granddaughter," chirps the woman,

a smile still on her face. Her eyes get all dreamy and wet. "Sarah was such a sweet girl."

"What happened to her?" I ask. My little sister's name is Sarah, but when Mom split, she took Sarah with her. Left me with my dad who spent more time stinking drunk than anything. He drank himself to death at forty-three. Sometimes though, through his booze stupors, he'd cry for Mom. I stopped crying for both of them a long time ago.

"Sarah died last year in a car accident. She was fourteen. Like you, she had her whole life ahead of her."

I start to laugh, but my gut feels all quivery and sick. I look away, thinking of my sister and realize it would be good to see her again. She lives in Idaho with Mom. I get a crazy idea that I should go see her. She's the only person who's ever cared about me.

I look at the old woman, who's still smiling, and my gut aches again.

"I'm sorry," I whisper, not sure where the words are coming from. "My sister's name is Sarah. She's sixteen now."

To my surprise, the old woman reaches out with claw-like, twisted hands and pats my arm.

I let her touch me. Her fingers are cold and rough and my first instinct is to pull away, but I force it down. I'm surprised that we have something in common. God, that's strange.

"Mrs. Sanderson is part of the test," says Mary Margaret. She points to the box sitting beside the water pitchers. It's about the size of an alarm clock. A red-haired woman, one of ones in scrubs, walks to the box and records some numbers.

"Bev, this is Kip, my new—" Mary Margaret looks at me for a moment and doesn't say anything.

"Felon," I say.

Mary Margaret's face twitches. "Kip, that's not what I—"

"It's okay," I say. "I know what I am."

For a few moments, no one says a word, but then the red-haired woman, Bev, turns toward me. "Kip, these monitors are recording data from each patient, so it's very important that they are working properly at all times."

I frown. "So you want me to check the boxes? Make sure they're all still working?"

Bev smiles, but it's not like Carmen's fake smile. "Exactly. When we have a complete set of data, we're going to compare the levels at time of death for any changes. And maybe identify some part of the soul."

"But why do you bother?" I ask. Who cares if it exists or not?

"The soul is our essence, Kip. When everything else breaks down, our soul is who we are inside. If we can prove it exists, then maybe death won't be so scary."

I've never thought about death being scary before. "How will you know if anything changes?"

"A good question," says Bev. She taps a small light on the front of the box. "If the numbers fluctuate significantly at time of death, then this indicator will flash. It may not prove anything, but the difference will be worth investigating."

The weeks slip into months and I find that these stiffs aren't the pains in the ass I thought they'd be. Nobody whines or complains much, but in their faces I see pain. Bev talks to me sometimes, asking me if I've had any trouble with the boxes.

Mary Margaret has had me eating lunch with her for weeks now. She's really not so bad. She tells good stories. And she's made me sit with Mrs. Sanderson every day. She's not so bad either.

"Sarah loved to play sports," says Mrs. Sanderson, her hand on mine. "Especially soccer. Do you play sports?"

"None that are legal."

Mrs. Sanderson laughs and for a moment the shadows on her face fade a little. I can almost see what she was like before she came here, but when the gray returns, I know she's dying. She looks past me now. I glance over my shoulder, but nobody's there.

"I'm not going to be here long," she says suddenly.

My throat tightens. "Why do you say that?" I don't like to hear her say that.

"I've seen her a few times—my Sarah. Once in the middle of the night. Yesterday, by the window." Her gaze is so far away. "And just now, behind you. My husband, Harry, too. I'm not scared. I'm ready to go. They're waiting for me."

I think of her Sarah, then I can't help but think of that guy —the one Donny killed. The events of that night in the alley come rushing back to me. Pounding through my brain in still life, frame-by-frame images. Almost like I can stop it. Almost.

Donny holds the gun and I'm rifling through the guy's pockets. He's tall and dark, his suit expensive. "Don't make me kill you, man," Donny growls, his face all wild and flushed. "Just give me the money." Freeze-frame.

The wallet's in my hands now, soft black leather smelling old and kind of like cedar. The money's crisp and stiff. Creased pictures hide behind the bills. His dark eyes hold mine in an unnatural stare and I smell his sour fear. He trembles beneath his black overcoat. His gaze flicks from Donny to the gun, to me and I start to laugh. His fear makes me feel important. Someone's giving me their undivided attention.

I hold out the wallet to him, displaying my prize, daring him to challenge me. Freeze-frame.

The words hang hollow in my ears. "Please," the man's voice quivers. "Take the money, just don't kill me!"

I laugh and run my hand down Donny's arm. I feel drunk —delirious. I like the echo of my voice in the alley. I like that I hold all the cards. Freeze-frame.

The gun barrel shadows in the glint of light from an over-head window as Donny raises the gun from his hip. It's sleek and black. Donny grins.

The guy's nostrils flare. His eyes widen. His whole body winds tight, his hands out, fingers spreading. His lips purse, a raw, desperate noise escaping.

Donny leers at the guy. He licks his lips, his eyes hungry.

Pop! God, the noise sounds so fake. Like a kid's toy. The guy jerks backward, his body flailing against the wall as his back comes apart. It all moves so slow, so surreal. Blood hits my cheek. I want to kick him. The dumbass made Donny shoot him. I stand there staring at him as he slides down the wall in a smear of blood. I want to scream and shake him.

Tears track down my face, the ache in my gut burning and throbbing. I double over, feeling so sick. It all seems so unreal now and all I can think about is that wallet. I never even looked at those pictures, but I think about them now. I wonder what he left behind that night. What we took from him that night. I shudder, thinking of my folks and Sarah. Mrs. Sanderson and her granddaughter.

And for the first time, I feel bad. I feel so bad. It was our fault. I know that now and it makes me gag. What if it had been this old lady? Or Mary Margaret?

Mrs. Sanderson's hand is still on mine. Mary Margaret is staring at me, saying nothing.

"Are you all right, Kip?" she asks finally, quietly.

I can't speak and I don't want them to see me cry, but dammit, I just can't help myself. I shake my head and rise from the bed, my arms folded against my stomach, and I run toward the bathroom.

Dry heaves rip through my gut. I drop down in front of a toilet. Again and again, I wretch air, but the sickness lies in my stomach like a rock. No matter what, I can't get rid of it.

Hands touch my shoulders and I jump, starting to pull away, but a voice fills my ears.

"You're okay," says Mary Margaret in a soft voice. "They told me this would be the hard part of your service. It'll get better. Facing our mistakes is hard, but you'll get through it."

I wretch again, but I don't try to pull away from her. Finally, my stomach settles and I lean against the wall. Mary Margaret kneels beside me, studying my face as she waits for me to say something. For a long time, I can only stare at her.

"I've seen that night a lot of times in my head," I say, "but not like I did today."

She squints at me. "What was different?"

I bite my lip. "This time, I cared." My throat feels tight again and my voice thins. "That guy in the alley. We just killed him like he was nothing. Like it didn't matter." I suck in a breath of air, thinking again of Mrs. Sanderson's Sarah—my sister, Sarah. "Like he didn't matter."

"It will be bad for a while, but then the pain will start to fade."

I frown. "How do you know?"

"Because we all have guilt, Kip. A little bit is healthy. Keeps us humble."

It's all new to me. I can only shrug.

"C'mon," Mary Margaret says with a grunt and rises to her feet. "Let's go check on some of the other residents."

Slowly, I get to my feet and I follow her into the bunkroom. She looks a bit thinner in the waist. She puts an arm around my shoulder and I remember a time when Mom use to do that. Mary Margaret isn't so bad.

———

I've been checking the boxes for a few weeks now, the rush of numbers and quiet little beeps confusing. I've never dealt with something like this before, but I do my work. I fill all the pitchers and straighten the beds. Mary Margaret hasn't been around much lately, always locking herself away in her office to deal with paperwork. I'd never admit it, but I miss her being around. Carmen's come to check up on me twice now, spending a lot of time with Mary Margaret. Every time I see her, my hackles raise. I wonder what Mary Margaret's telling her about me. Part of me doesn't care, but sometimes, I think about it and I get mad.

Mrs. Sanderson kicked off three weeks ago and that stupid box didn't show anything different. Mary Margaret says that nothing changed. She doesn't seem too bummed over the results. She's more upset over losing Mrs. Sanderson. But I'm not. Mrs. Sanderson wanted to go. She'd told me that nearly every day that she was ready, but Mary Margaret cries a lot and seems real messed up by the whole thing. I try to tell her

Mrs. Sanderson was okay with it, but she doesn't want to listen. She calls me callous and tells me to fill the water pitchers. I swear, with all this pitcher filling, I'm going to drown these people before my CS is over.

When I finish, I wander out of the bunk room. Light from Mary Margaret's door shines into the dim hallway ahead and I move toward it. The door is partway open, but I hesitate, trying to gather my words and hoping I don't say something stupid.

"Mary Margaret," I say finally and poke my head into the room.

It's dark except for the scalding desk light. She sits there unmoving with her head in her hands.

"What is it, Kip?" she asks, her voice weary. "I'm not in the mood for your antics today." Her face looks thin.

"I just wanted to tell you I'm sorry you miss Mrs. Sanderson so much. She wanted to go, you know. She said it's cool because she has people waiting for her."

Mary Margaret wipes her eyes with her hand and stares at me for a moment. Finally, she smiles. "Thank you, Kip."

I nod, feeling uncomfortable again, and start to slip out of the room, but she calls me back.

"It isn't just losing Mrs. Sanderson that I'm crying about," she says, her voice steady.

"Is it the experiment?"

Mary Margaret shakes her head slow and there's something in her eyes that sends a jolt of fear through me. Like she's given up or something. That look scares me. I saw it in that guy in the alley.

"No, I'm just being selfish, I guess. See, Mrs. Sanderson had cancer." Tears drip down her wrinkled face. "And so do I.

They gave me six months and I've been around a year now. My luck's about run out, too, Kip." She sighs. "I wanted to be here, to help you through your service."

Damn her! I want to slap her face. Just another one-way ticket. "It doesn't matter," I say in the calmest voice I can manage. Damn Mary Margaret for making me like her. "I don't need anybody's help."

"Anybody? No. You need somebody. Somebody who can reach you and so far, I'm it, kid."

"They'll just send me someplace else," I say. "I'll be okay, like always." She's leaving me—like everybody else. I turn toward the door, hiding my face from her. If I look at her I'm going to cry and then she'll know how much I care.

"I care what happens to you, Kip. We're making progress and I don't want it to stop." Her voice sounds so warm and concerned. I choke up, my throat hot and aching.

I drop down in the chair and fight against the sting in my eyes. "I don't care, do you hear?" I cross my arms and chant the phrase over and over to myself, but the tears slip down my face. Damned rehab.

She moves around the desk, her breathing heavy, and puts her hand on my arm. I jerk away.

"I trusted you!" I shout, my voice raw. I glare at her, but my bottom lip begins to quiver. I sink into the chair. "I don't want you to die," I say, the tears choking me.

Her eyes are watery as she puts her arms around me. My shoulders heave and everything spews. I can't hold it back. I tell her about my mom and Sarah and how I don't care about anyone, but she just holds me. Maybe she doesn't believe me?

"I'm not making this up," I say.

"I know," says Mary Margaret, her voice steady. "I'm just

glad you're trusting me with the story. I do care, Kip. Please believe me. I care what happens to you."

Silence is all I can respond with. No one's ever said that to me before. "See, I'm going to need your help very soon," she says. "You'll need to check all the monitors thoroughly, including mine. It's important to me, especially now. Promise you'll take care of this for me."

With a nod, I rise from the chair and excuse myself. I feel sicker than I have since my rehab session.

———

Two more people die over the next couple of weeks, but Bev's boxes don't seem to record any differences. Each time, Mary Margaret gets all depressed and quiet. Finally, one morning, I'm filling pitchers when Bev taps me on the shoulder, startling me.

"Kip?" she says, her eyes wide and her face pale.

"What is it?" I ask.

"Mary Margaret's ill," she says, her voice quiet.

All the air rushes out of my lungs. I try to take a deep breath and pretend like I don't care, but I can't do that anymore. Damn this thing in my head! I count the seconds to myself and try to hold it all together.

"Where is she?" I ask finally.

Bev points to the doorway. Mary Margaret's slumped there, one of the hospice workers and some of the researchers hanging over her. Just standing there gawking and not doing a damn thing to help. I hurry across the room and shove through them.

"Either help or get out of the way!" I shout. They move.

I force a smile to my lips as I bend down to Mary Margaret. "Hey, why you laying around when there's so much stuff to get done?" I ask.

She returns my smile, but she's so weak, so thin. "Kip, I need your help."

"You need somebody's wallet ganked?"

A thin laugh slips through her teeth as I put my arms around her waist and haul her to her feet. I keep my arm around her as we walk toward the empty bed near the bathroom. There's a window across from the bed, at least, so she can see outside. I've known for a while that Mary Margaret would end up here. It's an awful long walk and I wish we weren't making it. My gut feels quivery and hurts, a different sort of hurt this time. An empty feeling. God, it hurts.

I help her under the covers. Then I drop down beside the bed, feeling stupid, but part of me doesn't care anymore.

"Kip," she answers, her voice wheezy and thin. "Check my monitor. Want to—make sure it's working."

I fumble behind the thing and press a test button. It lights green.

"It's fine. What happened?"

"I'm not feeling well. Started late last night. I'm not going to be here long."

How does she know that? How did Mrs. Sanderson know? I swallow hard. Did that guy in the alley know?

"I'm scared, Kip."

My eyes sting. I reach out and put my hand on hers, squeezing. "It's okay," I tell her. "Mrs. Sanderson saw all those people waiting for her, remember. There's got to be a regular crowd waiting for you. Isn't that better than one of those dumb ol' boxes flashing at you?"

Her eyes get all weepy and her voice sort of chokes out. She nods.

My gut aches so bad and my hands tremble. It's all so much harder when you care, but I'm no coward. She's done it for all these people. I'll do it for her. "I'll stay with you as long as you want me."

"I'd like that," she says. Her face is droopy and gray, like Mrs. Sanderson's before she died. I feel so scared, but I'm not going to leave her now. I've got to let her know that I'm her friend and that I'm glad for everything she's done for me.

"See, besides Donny, I've never had a friend. They tell me Donny's not my friend, but he's all I've ever known." I force myself to smile. "Now, I got comparisons." My throat tightens, my eyes burning, and I can barely talk. "Thank you, Mary Margaret."

"Thank you, Kelly," she says, and I choke up. Mom used to call me Kelly when I was little. I became Kip when she took Sarah and moved away. I wipe back tears from my eyes.

"I'm not religious and I don't know about souls or what happens when we die," I say, my voice all shaky now, "but if you see that guy—the one in the alley…that we killed…would you tell him I'm sorry? Really sorry?"

She nods. "You're going to be all right."

———

The hours pass and the grayness hugging the edges of her face spreads. Her eyes look weak and her breathing's so shallow. Outside, the grayness settles around the place, like everything will just blot her out and she'll fade away. My hand is still holding hers, but it's been some time since she's squeezed it. I glance over at the box. What will it record? Will that light flash when she dies?

Bev walks over and adjusts some sort of monitor attached to Mary Margaret's temple and another attached to her chest. She pats me on the shoulder and walks away.

Toward afternoon, Mary Margaret begins to mumble, but I can't tell what she's saying. Even if I lean down, the words are too soft. I wonder what she's going on about, but I'll never know, I realize.

As afternoon slips away, so does Mary Margaret. Her chest rattles. It's a hollow sort of damp sound. Her breathing's fading. I rise from my chair, but I hold onto her hand. With her other hand, she reaches up at something I can't see. Slowly, the rise and fall of her chest lessens until finally, it just stops.

I glance at the box on the table beside the bed. Nothing. No flash, no light. Only a soft hum comes from the other monitor.

I let go of her hand and stand in front of the window, my knees shaky. Behind me, I hear feet pounding across the room. A faint alarm sounds from the flat-lined monitor. I try to tune it out. Two women in scrubs huddle beside Mary Margaret as they try to revive her.

I stare at the intense blue-green of the Pacific Ocean against the rocky shore. They won't be bringing Mary Margaret back. She's cast her soul to the sea.

Maybe, just about that, Donny is right? I think I understand his words now. And Bev's, too.

Over the ocean, thick, gray clouds part and sunlight pours down on the water. The light is almost white, the flickering so bright I squint and my eyes burn. Then it fades into the grayness again. I glance at the box. Dark. Silent.

I don't need that box to flash or anything else right now.

All I need now is time. And when it feels right, there's a trip I need to take. I'd like to tell Sarah about the mistakes I've made. But most of all, I'd like to tell her about Mary Margaret and this place—Mary Margaret's spirit house. At least, this is where I found mine.

ALL THINGS MUST END
SCOTT EDELMAN

Scott Edelman is a veteran writer and editor. Scott was the editor of the science fiction magazine <u>Science Fiction Age</u>. He published and edited the semi-professional magazine Last Wave from 1982 to 1985, which I sent stories to, but could never sell him a story even though I tried a bunch.

Other magazines edited by Edelman over the years include Sci-Fi Universe, Sci-Fi Flix, and Satellite Orbit. He became the editor of <u>SCI FI Magazine</u> (the official print magazine of <u>The Sci Fi Channel</u>) in 2002, and has edited the channel's online magazine <u>Science Fiction Weekly</u> since 2000.

But he did write some for the early years of Pulphouse, (yes, he has been around as long as I have) and now, his fifth story in this new incarnation is a pure Pulphouse story that I really thought fit right here in this anthology.

For more information about Scott's writing and editing, go to <u>www.scottedelman.com</u>

ALL THINGS MUST END

SCOTT EDELMAN

We didn't know where the strings came from -- they simply appeared one day, rising from where they'd suddenly looped around our wrists, necks, and ankles -- and wherever we happened to be in that shared moment of their manifestation, when we raised our heads to seek out where they led -- of our own volition, we believed, not tugged upward in any way by the sudden yoking -- we could see no end to them.

Those five strings -- thicker than thread, thinner than rope, smooth as silk, and one indistinguishable from another -- shot up vertically from each of us until they at some point seemed to converge and then vanish beyond what was visible by even the sharpest human eye.

We had no idea what waited at their other ends.

We had no idea if there even *were* other ends.

That ignorance did not sit well with us, any of us, so we looked for what we could not see.

I've been speaking of the effects of that strange day as a <u>we</u>

thing, as happening to us, and the reason is, I realize, so I won't have to think too much about me. No surprise there, as thinking that way has always been part of my nature. It long ago became clear to me -- that's what led me to choose my somewhat solitary career and my mostly solitary life.

I wasn't avoiding myself in that manner during the initial longing for a cause as to what occurred that day, though. My concerns then were no different than all of our concerns. And so it was not submerging myself to say we looked skyward. And when we did --

Binoculars couldn't find the ends of those strings. Neither could radar. And when the military sent drones aloft to seek the source, they discovered the strings continued way outside our atmosphere and far beyond the limits of their mechanical perception. What segments could be seen of the lower portions of the strings to which we were attached, however, showed they radiated outward, parting slightly and slowly, as if the Earth were the center of the universe. Even our finest telescopes could only reveal that those ever-widening lines extended up and up ... and higher still ... escaping the solar system and traveling beyond the known planets seemingly forever so their ends could not at all be seen -- even though all things must end.

We had no awareness the strings which bound us ever attempted to exert control. None we could perceive, anyway. We each experimented in our own ways to uncover whether that was so, and found we were allowed to move freely, without the loops which could not be loosened pulling us to the left or right, prodding us in one direction or another. We felt no tension to our connections, they were just ... there ... following. So we did not feel we were captives. We could live our lives on our own terms, without leading the lines along, without being led. Our momentum and inertia remained our own, our free will unsullied.

Regardless of that freedom, some attempted during that beginning to cut themselves away and back to the pre-event form of freedom which had existed throughout human history, applying scissors and fire, chainsaws and acid, and for the most desperate -- their own teeth gnawing furiously. But none were successful at releasing that invasive touch. As for me, I never tried to copy their efforts, even though no punishment came for those who did. I'd spent so much of my time alone, their presence was almost welcome. I felt an odd comfort there, one similar to what I felt when considering the fish tanks in the front waiting room -- a low key infectious serenity, ever present, and making few demands.

Besides, we could still go about our business. The strings did not prevent those of us who'd become tethered while out and about from returning inside, though many let fear prevent them from even making the attempt, which left them waiting until others tried and survived. Working at a mortuary as I'd been doing for five years before the strings first made their appearance had freed me of many fears, that to my surprise being one of them. Once any of us passed through a doorway, the strings would follow, continuing to hover straight above us, vanishing into whatever ceiling we were beneath, remaining taut as if a fishing line tossed into a pond hanging above our heads. And if another went outside to inspect, they'd find the strings continuing out of the roof and disappearing into the sky as usual, our homes and offices no barrier to the lines which -- if the news reports were to be believed -- harnessed every human being on Earth.

When it became clear the strings weren't going away any time soon, and were doing nothing (so far as we could tell) to interfere in our affairs, we did our best to move on, to live the lives we'd led before. Those of us who could, returned to our routines. As for others -- some changes were unavoidable.

Our planet, for instance, became smaller. Commercial flights were halted. Not because they were impossible, but because they'd become ... uncomfortable. Those who first dared to fly after the phenomenon began were unsettled by what the skies held for them. The skeins which thrust upward were inescapable even tens of thousands of feet in the air, and dodging them over all but the most desolate of areas was an impossibility for even the most skilled pilot. But after the first few times the paths of strings and planes crossed, we learned such acrobatics were not necessary to prevent damaging collisions, for the encounters caused no harm, gave no resistance whosoever. All that manifested, in fact, was a tickling within the pilots and passengers who personally passed through the strings belonging to another. It caused such a disorientation -- and created so many rumors the effect might be even more terrifyingly existential -- that the customer base evaporated and flights were soon grounded.

Car travel was up, though, making my life busier as a consequence, which I should have guessed would happen, considering my familiarity with the actuarial tables. That left me with little time to obsess about the new world in which we lived, a dual benefit -- what was good for business was also good for my peace of mind.

Every once in a while, someone would attempt to climb their strings -- which regardless of what those flying discovered up above, kept their solidity in such circumstances down below -- to see whether they could learn from where they'd been cast. They believed the previous inability of seekers to find an answer via radar, telescope, and the like, was because anything but the most natural of means was inevitably doomed to fail to reach whatever was on the other end of the strings. I could have told them what they were doing was pointless, that whatever answer waited out there really didn't matter and would affect no change in their lives, but I didn't even try. That would have been pointless, too.

They'd bring food and water with them, blankets for the cold they expected would come if they successfully rose, and hammocks which would enable them to pause along the way and sleep at the end of each day. Those of us too wise to fall for such foolishness would sometimes gather below to look on each time a person mounted such a pilgrimage, which resulted in so many of our strings condensing so tightly they'd block the sun, forcing the watchers to live in shadow until we grew bored and abandoned providing an audience for the impossible. Those few who chose to remain would watch the climbers rise until they vanished out of sight, never to be seen again, which unfortunately encouraged others, who wondered if their disappearances meant they found what they'd sought.

I was never one of them.

Never one of those who felt they should follow, that is. I was content with the new world. I did join the world in wondering, however. Just not about the same thing everyone else seemed to.

Here's the question I would often ask myself and have never been able to answer —were the strings truly newcomers to our existence, suddenly substantiating with no warning, giving no clue as to the event approaching, with a not there/there disconnect? Or had they always been with us, only we simply had never been able to see them before?

We all had different questions, it seems, and attempted to answer them in different ways.

Some were driven in their desperation to find the answers to their own questions by climbing the strings of others, to varying results. They would knock down strangers, then leap for their strings, feeling the less familiar tethering would give them a better chance of ascending than those who climbed their own. These unfortunate assaults seemed to happen most frequently to those who were pregnant, from whom a second set of strings rose, the theory being, I suppose, that any climb would have greater support upon ten strings than five. But whether the invaders would hurl themselves at one set of strings or two, most faced failure, for they'd pass through as if the lines weren't there at all, and hit the ground on the other side, where they'd lie dazed, sometimes unable to rise again for days, and not because of any injury, but rather ... they seemed to lack the will. A few managed to maintain contact and move upward -- and we never understood why those few were able when most could not. This connection to the strings of a stranger had little seeming effect on the one below, who would eventually get up from the attack and move about their day. As with all climbers, we never did find out what happened to those who rose.

Those were not the only methods the malcontents sought to break away from the world they'd been handed. There were some who leapt from tall buildings, hoping their strings would stretch like a rubber band, storing the energy needed to snap them back past where they'd begun and off into the heavens. Neither of those things ever occurred -- a number of the deceased were brought to me to deal with after -- so it didn't happen as often as you might suppose. Others would go deep sea diving, believing that if they descended deep enough their strings would snap. What they thought would happen next if they were to have been released, I never learned, but as it never happened, the results being more tragic than triumphant, it didn't really matter.

So most of us continued on, neither seeking answers nor seeking to be set free by them, living our lives and trying to forget the strings were even there. And after awhile, it was almost as if they weren't. On the right days, in the right moods, they were almost invisible, like those floaters in the corners of one's eye which can for the most part be forgotten except on the brightest of sunny days.

I was lucky enough to be one of those. Though perhaps it had little to do with luck, but rather the inescapable influence of my circumstances.

As I went about my work, preparing my unfortunate customers for the next world, two things happened -- I saw firsthand the results of those who'd struggle to escape their fates -- and by bearing witness I surrendered to whatever my own was meant to be. My job at the funeral home had me privy in a way most others were not to what came after, so I knew -- not even death could cut the strings. As the bodies were laid out, the lines which bound them still rose to whatever in the sky kept them tethered. Cremation did not sever the ties, either, for I could see the strings rising from those who chose that path, so close together as to be indistinguishable, connecting the urn to the heavens. Walking the cemetery grounds every day and seeing strings leaving the grass to pierce the clouds changes a person, in a way spending one's time only around the tethered living does not, and it told me there was no escape either in this life or the next. So I knew not to try.

Unlike many industries which were either curtailed or eventually shut down entirely -- such as private detectives, and the manufacturers of night vision goggles and home pregnancy tests -- I remained fully and increasingly employed, the incursion having no negative effect on my life, and then not directly. It was merely ripples from those more acutely affected. People had been dying long before the strings arrived, and continued to die (albeit at a slightly higher rate) while they were here, so my skills, as mundane as they were, remained necessary. And after they left, if they left, they'd be necessary still.

But would there be an after? From time to time, I would look to the sky and wonder.

But with no answers in sight, I told myself it did not matter. As I said, I had chosen to surrender. (Or thought so.)

Accepting as I was (or told myself I was) of the new order to things, and no longer longing for release, I ignored my bonds, the ones (as I have said) I often forgot were even there, unlike those forever conscious of wanting the old ways back. Which meant my first notice that things were about to change was a slight heaviness in one of my wrists as I stretched out my hand to button the collar of a man who had passed the previous night. My fingers missed their target, colliding with the old man's chin, and when I jerked back my hand I noticed --

There was suddenly a slack to the string, as it no longer leapt straight up from the top of my wrist, but had begun to droop down below. And then I saw what wrapped around my other wrist was the same, and the strings at my ankles had already dropped so severely the curves of them now draped to the floor.

Screams erupted from outside, and I stepped to the street, for the first time feeling a resistance, and once I'd dragged myself to the sidewalk I could hear the sound of a distant whistling.

The streets around the funeral home were relatively quiet, and what few pedestrians there were had become trapped where they stood, frozen by the spirals which had begun to loop around their feet. I made to move toward the closest, but couldn't, then looked down to see my own strings gathering there. It was as if whatever had held the other end in place had let go, allowing them to fall. Or had they been cut rather than released? Whichever they had been, they continued to fall, the whistling increasing in intensity and causing an ache in my ears as they did so.

Though the mounds grew higher, the nature of the strings themselves appeared unchanged, and when I looked up, what remained above still stretched far beyond my sight, this relatively slight gathering having no change on whether I could see a beginning or end.

Someone nearby cried out for help, and when I tried to do just that, I instead pitched forward, tripping over the barrier which had by then risen past my knees. I fell on my side and rolled to my back, but when I tried to rise again, I was unable to move, for such a weight of falling strings had amassed against my chest, I was pinned. What had for so many months been ethereal and undemanding had become quicksand, and I could do no more than watch and listen while the whistling transformed into a dull rumble as if a thunderstorm were racing toward me.

I couldn't even turn my head, but what strings I was able to see still stretched to infinity. I hoped this meant, the fall by the sound of it picking up speed, that I'd soon see the end of things, but that was not to be, for the strings began to criss-cross my face until my eyes were soon covered, and then I could see no more.

The darkness quickly became the least of my concerns, as the accumulated weight across my chest of what had once been weightless made it difficult to breath. I was uncertain, even as I struggled, whether we were being set free or abandoned, and my emotions vibrated between gratitude and betrayal. I no longer remember which of those feelings was strongest as I lost consciousness.

When I eventually came to, still on the sidewalk where I'd fallen, the strings were gone, the skies were clear, and I was alone. I must have been the last to rouse, for the others had all gathered themselves and gone. Many hours had clearly passed, for it was night. I could see the stars, and looking upon them could not remember having ever seen so many at once. Did that mean there were really more than there once had been, perhaps birthed by what we had endured? Or had their existence merely been blocked for so long, my memory of them could not compete with their reality? As I waited for the effects of my smothering to fully pass, I thought about those stars, and those who might live on the other planets which could be circling them. I wondered whether somewhere out there another to whom I had once been connected lay on their back as newly untethered as I was, and what their release might mean to them.

But those questions were as meaningless as any of the others, and so I rose and returned to my back office, where I completed dressing the old man for his funeral. I assumed others elsewhere were also getting on with their lives.

But not all of them, I was later to learn. Some, in response to the moment, abandoned their families and jobs, fearing the strings might return with as little warning as their initial appearance, and hoping they could outrun the inevitable and hide from what awaited them. Others never even got back to their feet, but simply lay where they had fallen and starved. Then there are the ones who longed for them back, longed for the touch which had, if not guided us, at least accompanied us. Comforted us.

I became one of those, though I was not one at first. But as I moved through the world to which we've been told we've returned, I came to realize ... we've returned to nothing. I now understand the reason we never felt the weight of the strings upon us, never felt them urge us this way or that, never felt them holding us back, neither encouraging nor chastising, was that no guidance was ever necessary. It's simple, you see? All is foreordained, so what need was there to control when we always do as we are meant to do? The choices I understood to bring me here? An illusion. To believe in free will is to believe in a lie. That is what they existed to teach us, and having taught us, whether we learned their lesson or not, left.

And that is why you find me like this, with strings I myself have wrapped around my wrists and ankles, and another about my neck. They don't reach for the sky as the other hd. In fact, they exist only a few inches beyond each of the five knots I have made. But I want the universe to hear me, to know that even if no one else has listened, I at least have learned.

And if the universe does not hear, does not respond -- and why would it, having said all I fear needed to be said? -- I have a rope waiting, one far thicker than either the strings I've just used or the earlier five which once bound me. It's long enough -- just long enough and no more -- to take me where the lessons have shown me I choose to go next.

AFTER
ANNIE REED

Professional writer Annie Reed writes stories that span genres and are always powerful. In fact with Annie, you just never know the type of story you might be reading, but you will always know it will grab you and be a compelling read.

So far Annie has had a story in every issue of Pulphouse magazine and as the editor, I hope to continue that streak.

Annie's stories have appeared in four best mystery stories of the year volumes so far. Look for so much more of Annie's work at her website https://anniereed.wordpress.com/

AFTER

ANNIE REED

The older Belle Creedy gets, the more she wonders about what happens. After.

In the mornings, when dawn's just a lick of peach in the eastern sky and she's so far into the world of her art she only knows the sun's coming up because the racket from the birds roosting in the thick pines around her house intrudes on her thoughts, she stops whatever she's working on and pads out onto the deck on the second story of her place. She watches ripples on the surface of the clear mountain lake just across the road take on the color of the pre-dawn sky, and she considers just how many coincidences go into making a world like this. Are they really coincidences after all? Or is there something more?

It's quiet this morning, so early in the day the birds have barely started their chatter. So early that Gary Weeds, another old-timer like herself, isn't even on the lake yet. Gary lives halfway up the mountain. He fishes every day he can, and since he retired in 1989, he can fish almost every day the weather lets him. He crunches down the one-lane dirt road that snakes up through the pines, rod and tackle box in his hand, and shoves off in his rowboat. Sits out on the lake half the day, the damn fool. One of these days she's gonna catch Gary peeing over the edge of his boat. Man has a cast iron bladder, but even a cast iron bladder can't stand against the ravages of time.

No one's on the lake yet. She can hear the shallow waves slapping up against Gary's boat where he moored at the end of the pier just as clear as if the boat and water were in the next room. Sound carries good out here, the air as crisp and clean as a new day should be.

Her hands ache this morning, the puffy joints of her fingers stiff and sore. "Storm blowing in," was what her mother would say. Maybe she'd be right, but this morning the sky only has a hint of clouds far to the north.

Her mother would have known the names of all the birds that live in the pines and cedars and tall birch trees. Known their names and catalogued each sound by type and volume. A good keeper of records, her mother was. Belle's not nearly as neat or concerned. She only knows that she likes the chirps and twitters, likes to imagine the conversations going on from nest to nest, punctuated with a sudden flutter of wings as effectively as she underlines words in her drawings.

This place inspires her. She produces page after page of glimpses into a whimsical world her mother never could have imagined. A place where animals talk and people are seen only from the waist down as a collection of shoes and legs and feet that stand and walk and jog, oblivious to the world they tread upon.

The animals in her drawings are smart—not book smart,

but intelligent in a way that comes from observing things first-hand. Belle's had nearly three-quarters of a century doing the same thing. The animals she draws are parts of her, like she supposes writers are part and parcel of every character they write or composers leave a bit of themselves in every new song. Maybe that's the cost of living with only a small part of her head in this world of early morning quiet while most of her exists in the places she creates, worlds as real to her as old Gary's boat and tackle box.

She feels the characters in her head calling to her to come back and play, but she makes no move to leave the deck. She wraps an old fleece blanket around her shoulders to ward off the worst of the morning chill. She wants a cup of coffee, but she doesn't go inside to make that either. Soon enough she'll make the first coffee of the day, then she'll go downstairs and sink her aching fingers deep into the first dough of the day and knead it with the same enthusiasm she has for the past twenty years. She'll greet the first customer in the door of her little bakery with a smile and a nod because even in this out-of-the way spot, she has customers who appreciate things made by hand, not machine. For now, it's just her and the lake and the impending dawn, and her thoughts about what comes after.

What's upset her this morning, made her feel her mortality a little more than usual, is a memorial service for someone she never knew. Jerry Garcia's ashes were scattered the day before near the Golden Gate bridge in San Francisco. That's a good thousand miles away from where she stands on the second story deck of her place, but she feels the loss as keenly as if she was there, standing in the shadow of that famous bridge, watching as his ashes drifted into nothingness in the damp air.

Belle was never a Deadhead. She never even went to concerts much when she was a young girl. Some of her customers call her an old hippie because she's got tie-dye shirts for sale in her place right alongside loaves of bread and fancy pastries.

Was she a hippy? She never wore flowers in her hair, never puffed much less inhaled, and her love was never free. Her life, though—her life was always less than conventional. For long years she wandered from place to place, waitressing here, typing there, and always, always drawing. Vagabond, maybe that's what she was. A vagabond who set down roots too soon. She regrets never having gone to one of Garcia's concerts now that it's certain there will never been another.

She had a radio playing yesterday. She always does when she's making food. She can't get the lyrics of one of his songs out of her head. The station played it as a tribute, a salute to surviving from a man who, like the rest of the world, ultimately hadn't.

The grey in her own hair fools people into thinking she's normal, as if the only mental affliction that happens to the elderly is senility, not the imaginary-world not-thereness of creativity. Sometimes she draws a sketch on a clean paper napkin and gives it to a child along with a muffin or a cinnamon sweet roll. Her drawings paper the walls of her place, make the children giggle and adults smile indulgently. She wonders what will happen to the insightful animals in her world after she's gone. Will they be overlooked and trampled on by the nameless feet that shuffle and walk and march through their lives? Will they survive even if she doesn't?

She hopes someone will scatter her ashes across this lake, although she imagines after she's gone, where her remains are scattered won't matter much at all to her. Did it matter to Jerry Garcia? Maybe the animals she's spent most of her life drawing will care. She wonders what the animals in her world will say about her after she's gone, much like she wonders what they talk about while she's sleeping.

Far out across the lake, the dark shape of a bird glides close to the water. Not a pelican or a crane or one of the nesting eagles that live in the little island a quarter mile offshore. She's seen this before. Her doctor says it's just a dark spot in her vision, the harbinger of approaching blindness. She knows it's something else.

Dawn is approaching, she can feel it, see the glow in the eastern sky lighting up the glassy surface of the lake. Today the birds in the high pines aren't as chatty as they have been in days past. Maybe the dark bird on the water intimidates them. It should intimidate her, frighten her, but she's come to know it with every friend she's laid to rest, every scattering of ashes and fistful of dirt she's dropped in an open grave.

Did Jerry see the dark shape, too? Did he recognize it for what it was? She thinks it only comes for creative sorts, people who live their lives with one foot in the here and now and one in another place entirely. Maybe it's the thing that lives in the closet or under the bed in the world where her animals live, the thing that scares them, which is why they never talk to her about it, even though, lord knows, they talk to her about everything else.

She stands on the deck and watches the shape glide over the lake, closer now than it's ever been before. Her hands still ache with the early spring morning cold. Her nose is numb and her breath puffs out little clouds of mist. A bench table on her deck is decorated with a whimsical mermaid fountain she found once on a trip to Baja. The fountain doesn't work anymore, but she hadn't the heart to throw it out, so now the mermaid sits on the table and stares out across the lake much like Belle does. Do the mermaid's hands get cold? Does she long to feel herself glide beneath the surface, her strong tail propelling her far away from the unforgiving solidity of land?

And still the bird glides closer.

Belle thinks she can feel the bird now too, just like she feels the dawn, and she wonders if she'll make it until the sun comes up. Will Gary find her? Or will it be a customer, someone come for fresh bread and drawings or maybe a tie-dye shirt, and instead see Belle still up on the deck wrapped in a fleece blanket, here but not really here anymore.

She should be frightened. She's had a good long life, but when she got up from her drawing table to wander out on her deck, it wasn't with the knowledge that this would be her last dawn, the last time she looked out across the lake where she'd lived the last twenty years.

"Go on without me," she says in a voice that doesn't seem to have much substance. "Don't die with me."

A raccoon sits on its haunches on the ground below and takes notice, its sharp little nose twitching in the predawn air. The bird glides toward shore, and the raccoon whispers to her that it will miss her.

Was that why they scattered his ashes near the bridge? So that his spirit wouldn't die? Or so that the spirits he created would live on after his was gone?

"Remember me," she says to the raccoon. It disappears on a breath of air, leaving only a cold, empty expanse of grass in its wake.

Belle sits down on a wooden plank bench on her deck, the

blanket tight around her shoulders. She can't see her breath in front of her face anymore. Is she still breathing? Hard to tell. Maybe she's already gone.

She thought this transition would be the worst of all, but it's painless. She's remade herself so many times in her life—child to rebellious teenager, to wandering adult, to responsible store owner, and each transition came with its own brand of pain. Now she only feels numb and detached even from the melancholy that brought her out here on the deck to watch the dawn.

The black bird swoops low over the last of the trees standing post around her shop. It circles overhead once and then drops down to perch on the deck railing.

"Time to go," it says to her in a voice much like those of the animals she drew.

It holds out a wingtip. After hesitating only a moment, she reaches out to touch it. The feathers feel soft and as unsubstantial as a cloud to her frozen, arthritic fingers. "I'm ready," she says.

It smiles at her. It can't, of course, because it's a bird and birds don't smile, not even in the drawings and tales she's told herself, but this bird smiles. "Your friends are here," it says.

She looks over her shoulder. The sun has almost crested the mountains to the east. She can see her drawing table inside. All her animal friends are there—the raccoons and squirrels and chipmunks on the table, the brown bear and fawn standing next to each other on the floor. The regal moose, his antlers held high, stands tall on the other side. It feels good to know they haven't disappeared just because she's leaving. It's better to know that they're letting her go without tears.

"I'm ready," she says again, and smiles back at the bird.

She wanted to know what would happen. After. She imagined cold and dark and nothingness, or perhaps lifting toward an ethereal light, or maybe even drifting toward the stars. She imagined fear and sorrow at leaving everything behind. She never imagined joy.

Pain and cold and the stiffness of her body disappear as she sails off the deck on the tip of the bird's wing. Golden sunlight glints off the water beneath them, and as she looks down, she can see through the water like it was glass. She feels the water as if she was swimming through the depths of her lake rather than soaring above it.

She turns to look at the tall pines on the island where the eagles roost, and she can feel them in their nest, resting content with their bellies full of fish. She hears the trees sigh at the first light of dawn and feels the shift of gravel beneath Gary Weeds' old boots as he comes tromping down the dirt road.

"Survive," she says to the first puff of breeze across the lake. "I survive."

"Yes," the bird says. "All things do. Didn't you know?"

I'd hoped, she wants to say. "I thought I'd only be a memory," she says instead.

"The world is not that wasteful." The bird turns toward the north, leaving Belle's place behind. "Look," it says as it guides her higher. "See."

She wants to gasp at the beauty of it all. Her world, but not like she's ever seen it before. Experienced it before. She only got close in her imagination, when she glimpsed a small part of the connectedness of all things and listened when her animals talked.

This isn't After. Not the way she thought of it. Everything

else was Before. This is Now, and it is absolutely where she belongs.

"Show me more," she says.

And the bird did.

GRIEF SPAM

KRISTINE KATHRYN RUSCH

Kristine Kathryn Rusch is a New York Times *and* USA Today *bestselling writer and maybe the most award-winning and prolific writer working today. She has won more awards in science fiction and mystery than just about anyone alive and she is the only person to win the Hugo Award for her writing as well as her editing.*

This fantastic novella will grab you right from the start and not let you go.

It was also included in the The Mysterious Bookshop Presents The Best Mystery Stories of the Year 2022.

You can find out a lot more about Kris's work at her publisher, WMG Publishing Inc <u>www.wmgbooks.com</u> *or her website www. kriswrites.com*

GRIEF SPAM

KRISTINE KATHRYN RUSCH

Day sixteen since Rob's death, not that Lucca was counting—oh, hell, of course she was counting. The days, the hours, the minutes. She was counting everything because that was the only way to keep her brain focused.

But not focused well enough apparently, because she woke up that morning, like she had for the past fifteen mornings, reaching for Rob on his side of the bed, wondering why he had gotten up so early, wondering what day it was, wondering if she had forgotten to drive him to work, wondering—

And then she remembered. Sledgehammer, nightmare, emotionally devastating.

Those words didn't even describe it.

More like existing between being and nothingness. She rested on the soft king bed, pillow scrunched beneath her head, covers wrapped around her like a hug, the cats pressed against her as if they were afraid she would leave too, and let the reality sink in.

She used a trick, one she had developed ten days ago. She reviewed everything in her head.

She started with the obit, because she had had to write it, and she had the damn thing memorized:

Robert Zedder, 48, loving father and husband, died in a single car collision on Route 73, just outside Watersville. Beloved assistant principal of Anderson High School, Zedder had worked for the Watersville School District for twenty-five years. Recipient of Teacher of the Year for five years running, Zedder maintained his teaching career while working in the high school administration.

He leaves behind his wife, Lucca Kwindale, his daughters Annette, Sybil Washington, and Marla Zedder-James, and three granddaughters...

At which point, Lucca's throat ached—every single time. He would never see Annette graduate from college, never see the grandbabies grow, never see their babies, never see—

Lucca made herself sit up. The cats lifted their heads, startled, bits of their fur floating in the semi-light of the early morning filtering in the bedroom window. A bedroom on the east side of the house had been Rob's idea, since he had to get up early for school. Too early, she had always complained, and he would laugh.

Self-employed people don't understand schedules, he would say, and by that he would mean *she* didn't understand schedules, never realizing that self-employed people had to schedule better than anybody else, or no one would think they were working.

Old arguments, now irrelevant. Lucca ran a hand over her face. Day sixteen. He had died on a Tuesday (a Tuesday in April, four days before taxes were due, at four in the goddamn morning—what had he been doing driving at four in the goddamn morning?), which meant that this was Thursday, some mucky-muck day at the end of April, nearly May, which he used to say was his favorite month.

Mucky-muck day. She'd learned that phrase from him too. She had lived half her life with him—married at twenty-four—and she was having trouble separating herself from that. Having trouble figuring out how to move forward, how to think, even. Strangely, it had been easier in the first few days after his death because there had been—ironically enough—a schedule.

So, last night, she realized she needed a new schedule. The non-existent schedule, she would have said to him, had he still been alive, and she would have said it with a smile, and just enough sarcasm and bite to let him know she kinda resented the way he had minimized her work each and every day.

He would have heard the bite, and it would have made him defensive.

He was helping people, he would have said, teaching kids how to be good citizens, making sure the school ran well, working toward the future.

He hated her work. She didn't hate his, but she thought it was dreary.

She didn't see her work as noble—only private detectives in novels were noble—but she saw it as useful and interesting, and a whole hell of a lot less dangerous now that she did 90% of it online.

She and her crew. Her crew, who were taking point at the moment. Her crew, who probably needed some kind of pep-talk acknowledgment from her.

Later today, she would head to the office where the crew worked. She would give them an hour. She figured she could handle an hour without tears. Maybe an hour would give her enough focus to put her pesky emotions in their place.

She'd read about grief. Hell, she'd combed the web to find out everything she could about grief.

It's a process, the websites told her.

It's harder when things are left unsaid, the websites warned.

Be aware, they counseled. *The emotions come in waves.*

Emotions, not emotion. Not sadness, not mind-numbing despair. But sadness *and* mind-numbing despair. Anger *and* denial. Shock *and* acceptance. Depression *and* bargaining— wait. Bargaining with whom? With the idiot who was out driving at four in the morning on a school night? Who probably fell asleep behind the goddamn wheel, missed a turn, and slammed into a concrete abutment that was slated to be repaired by the Department of Transportation next summer, because the damn abutment was an accident magnet?

Whew. She let out a small breath. Anger. It billowed when she least expected it. She didn't think of herself as an angry person, but she certainly wasn't a calm one either.

Never had been, never would be.

She had made a list the night before, so she wouldn't have to think about her day. Thinking about the day, she believed, was what had paralyzed her this past week. Now that the funeral was over. Now that the girls had gone home to their separate cities, their separate lives, and their separate grief. Now that the planning was done.

Yeah, right. The lack of schedule had paralyzed her. Not the loss of Rob. Not that at all.

Lucca grabbed her robe from the chair beside the bed, slipped her feet into the worn slippers she'd meant to replace at Christmas, made a brief stop in the bathroom, avoided the kitchen where the cats were already gathering for their break-fast treats, and proceeded down the side hall to her home office.

A second master the builders had called it when they slapped this place together from custom pieces. She didn't care about what they called this part of the house. When she and Rob had looked for the perfect home to raise their family in, she had insisted on the home office, as far from the main living quarters as possible.

She just wanted—and got— two rooms and a bathroom to herself so she could have an outer office and an inner sanctu-ary. She even had her own entrance—very important in the early days, when (stupidly) she let the clients come here.

She had never told Rob about the guy who had threatened her at knife point, or the cheating wife who had shown up with a shaking gun in her right hand. Rob couldn't have done anything about it except worry. In his later years, he had put on weight around the middle, always intending to exercise, and never exercising at all.

If he had been alone with someone who had become violent because of her work, he wouldn't have been able to defend himself. He would have died, because of her. (Of course, this year, he had died because of him. Or the damn abutment. Or the stupid car.)

It had taken a knife and a gun, and a couple of threats left on her voice mail to wake her up. Fortunately, before anything had happened.

Before someone had gone after her family with evil intent.

That year—ten years ago now—Lucca had decided on an outside office, the farther away the better. Rob had complained bitterly, about the distance, the expense, the location—everything. Initially she thought he was being controlling—he didn't want her away from the house. Later, she thought maybe the outside office made her work even more embarrassing to him.

He thought of private detectives as blue collar. He'd once said, *What a waste of an education, Lucca. You were Phi Beta Kappa, second in a class of five hundred at one of the most prestigious universities in the nation. I tell my kids they want to achieve all those goals so they'll get the best jobs ever, not dig through someone else's underwear to see if it has holes.*

She'd walked away from him that day. Hadn't even fought back. They'd said a lot of ugly things to each other in their fights, but neither of them had ever walked away before.

And he knew—because he wasn't dumb (wasn't Phi Beta Kappa either, but wasn't dumb)—that if he kept pushing her like that, she would walk away for good.

So she'd got her outside office. Smartest decision she'd ever made, besides going back to school to learn the ins and outs of computer research. As the business grew, the offices grew, the staff grew, and she out-earned Rob by more than double.

Although, since she handled the family finances, he never knew that. He hadn't known a lot of things, because she'd stopped telling him.

There had been no point.

And now, he would never know. Her legs buckled at the thought. She put a hand on the wall, wondered if, now that he was dead, he actually did know. Maybe he knew everything now. Some cultures believed that consciousness spread all over time, learning life's lessons.

She made herself stand up, let go of the wall, keep moving.

She wasn't a weak person, no matter how she felt. She wasn't superhero strong, either, but she could move forward in the face of all difficulties.

Rob'd said once, after Annette was born, that he thought Lucca could give birth, then take a five-mile hike, and cook a six-course meal, all in the same day.

She didn't have that kind of stamina now—in fact, she couldn't remember the last time he had said something like that—but she was usually stronger than she had been these past sixteen days. Not the kind of woman who sobbed alone in her bedroom, with only her cats for company.

Lucca opened the hallway door into her office. The door led into the outer sanctum, once the reception, now a dump spot for old paper files, boxes, and photographs that should probably never see the light of day.

The inner office remained her home office, six different kinds of computers and two laptops, three routers, all hard-wired in, plus two different internet hot spots through two different companies. She did searches here that she didn't want on her office network, and she routinely cleaned off and dumped computers when she had stumbled on some truly perverted stuff in the course of an investigation.

Usually she used the client's computer for that, going through whatever they let her investigate, sometimes in her office, sometimes in their home. But she'd been doing this long enough that she got a sense of people, and she could tell if they were the kind who might make her life a living hell.

In the middle of the computer jungle was her personal laptop, the one she used for family emails and her private social media accounts—the ones only shared with her daughters, her extended family, and a handful of close friends. She made sure she bought a new laptop every year, something cheap and not very sophisticated, and carried it with her on vacations and in the car.

She liked to think of that computer as an extension of the woman who lived in this house, the woman who had married Rob, bore three children, and raised them in as old-fashioned a way possible. Sometimes she thought of that woman as the fictional version of herself, the one she presented to the family and to the neighborhood, not the hard-assed broad who knew when a client was lying to her, or who had talked down that guy with a knife.

She grabbed the computer out of her old leather recliner, the one piece of furniture in the entire house that predated everything, from her relationship with Rob to the move to this city. An old boyfriend had bought the chair for her, the only piece of furniture in her entire one-bedroom apartment. She'd slept in the damn chair for nearly three months, long after he had broken up with her.

Rob hadn't known where the chair came from, only that she wouldn't part with it because it had been in her first apart-ment. He hadn't asked more.

She sank into it, robe parting along her knees. She cradled the laptop to her chest, thinking about her future while all wrapped up in her past.

Well-made furniture often outlived the people who first owned it. Well-built houses did too. Stuff lived longer than people, than husbands, than true love.

Sometimes stuff held its secrets—like this chair—secrets that would die with her. And sometimes stuff broadcast the secrets far and wide, once the stuff had been found in a hidden compartment or in the back of a closet or tucked (forgotten) in the pocket of an old coat.

She used to love ironies like that.

She used to love a lot of things.

She shook off the thought, opened her laptop, and typed in her password. The screen bounced into life, informing her that she hadn't opened the laptop in seventeen days—a notification she set up for herself so that she would know when she'd neglected her personal life for much too long.

Seventeen days.

He'd been dead for sixteen.

She couldn't remember why she had been on the computer the day before his death. Probably checking Facebook, seeing what the girls were doing, looking at the pictures of her grand-babies, or maybe even downloading music for her marathon exercise sessions.

It all blurred.

She took a deep breath before opening her email program. She knew what she would find. Dozens (maybe hundreds) of condolences. Lots of offers of help—whatever that meant. Grief spam (a widowed friend had warned her about that). And way back, normal emails, the kind that had been sent Before, the kind that had assumed normal would continue, not just for hours, but for days, months, and years.

She clicked on the computer's built-in timer, set it for an hour, then opened the email program. One hour. If she didn't want to read the condolence letters she didn't have to. She could just spend that hour deleting the grief spam.

The email downloaded faster than she expected. Three hundred emails, according to the little bar, most of them from familiar names. She watched the subject lines change from mundane things to topics like *Thinking of You* and *Call Us If You Need Anything*.

And then, in the middle of it, emails from people she didn't recognize, with the subject lines in all caps.

THE TRUTH ABOUT ROBERT ZEDDER; SEE WHAT ROBERT ZEDDER HAD DONE IN THE DAYS LEADING UP TO HIS DEATH; DISCOVER WHO ROBERT ZEDDER REALLY WAS.

On and on and on. That wasn't the grief spam she had been expecting. She had expected (and gotten) *Meditation for Widows* (Jesus, she was a widow now), *Join Our Grief Community*, and *Avoid Scams Targeted at the Grieving* (she thought that particularly pernicious).

But the ones with Robert's name, those disturbed her.

She looked at the dates of the emails, saw they had come to her after the obituary was published (every-damn-where), and slammed the laptop closed.

Fucking predators. That was a particular kind of nasty that she would delete when she was calm enough. When she wasn't feeling like isolating and opening each email before sending malware directly to the sender. When she wasn't feeling like tracking down the IP and finding the person's exact address, and going there and—

She made herself breathe, again.

She set the laptop aside and stood. The timer would go off, but it wouldn't repeat, so she could just leave it.

She needed breakfast anyway.

After that, the kitchen felt like a haven, rather than a reminder of Rob's absence. Even though his favorite shoes sat haphazardly under the table in the breakfast nook, where he had taken them off the night before. Even though his nasty protein powders still cluttered up her granite countertop. Even though the mail was piled a bit too high on the island.

Light poured into the windows that surrounded the nook, and outside, leaves had sprouted on the trees that gave this part of the lawn so much privacy.

The three cats twirled and meowed on the tile floor, waiting for her to take care of them, which she did—the standard morning routine, the same as it had been a month ago—filling bowls, filling water, giving them a bit of soft food.

She followed the routine, because she had promised herself routine, poured some shredded wheat, dressed it up with fresh strawberries someone had left, added a side of peanut butter toast for protein, took her damn vitamins, and made coffee.

Routine.

Except she couldn't turn on the TV under the counter, couldn't open her tablet to see the news of the day, couldn't bear to do more than stare and eat. Finally, she picked up her phone, tapped it open—and found nearly a dozen texts and messages from her daughters.

The most recent came from Antoinette.

Mom! Where Are You?

Followed by one from Marla.

Mom, we're getting concerned.

And from Sybil.

Mother, you need to pick up the phone.

Lucca scrolled through before she did, not willing to be blindsided by anything, but afraid she might be.

Her phone vibrated in her hand. She had shut off the ringer days ago. The screen lit up: the call was from Antoinette.

Lucca leaned against the kitchen island, bracing herself,

gaze on the empty cat dishes still littering the floor, and answered the phone.

"Hey, baby girl," she said, as she always did when greeting her youngest.

"Mom. Where *were* you?" Antoinette's voice hadn't shaken like that since she was six, and broke her leg after falling out of a tree.

"I—um—." Lucca glanced at the clock on the microwave. It was eleven-thirty, much later than she usually got up. "I have been keeping the phone in the kitchen."

She had expected Antoinette to say something about that, but she didn't. Instead, Antoinette took an audibly shaky breath, and said,

"They're not true, are they? Those screen shots? They're made up, right?"

Screen shots? Lucca felt dizzy. Outside of the house, Rob was alive, handling the kids at school with his usual mixture of aplomb, severity, and humor, taking the small emergencies. He would have handled this, this call, the girls upset. He would have dealt with it, because he handled kids. All the kids.

"What screen shots?" Lucca asked, wishing she didn't have to.

"You haven't *seen* them? Mom, aren't you getting your email?"

Lucca's breakfast rolled in her stomach. Those emails— they had gone to her daughters.

"I downloaded it," Lucca said, "but didn't look at it."

Not really. Just enough to see those subject lines—*The Truth About Robert Zedder*.

The truth.

"You have to look, Mom." Antoinette's voice wobbled. "You have to do *something*. It can't be about Dad. It can't."

"It probably isn't," Lucca said as calmly as she could manage—more calmly than she expected, in fact. She was talking to her daughter now as if Antoinette were an unruly client. "A widowed friend of mine warned me about the email. She called it grief spam."

"And you didn't warn us?" Antoinette asked. "You should have warned us."

"I didn't think you'd get any," Lucca said. *I didn't think it would be personal, either,* she wanted to add. *With Rob's name and everything.* "I'll text your sisters and then take a look."

"It's awful, Mom," Antoinette said.

"I'll keep that in mind," Lucca said, and hung up.

She texted her other two daughters and told them to hold tight; she was investigating. They knew that investigating was one of Lucca's most serious words.

Then she headed back down the hall, clutching the phone, and bracing herself. Antoinette said the spam was awful, but it couldn't be worse than identifying Rob's body through that stupid camera at the morgue, or looking at his embalmed but broken face, and calmly agreeing with the mortician that the casket should remain closed.

Lucca was braced—and weirdly, a little relieved. Something to do. Not make-work. Not work for the sake of work.

Something that mattered. For her girls.

Lucca set the phone on the side of her big desk, then grabbed the laptop off her leather chair. She pulled back her desk chair, and sat down, placing the laptop in the center of all the equipment.

She'd done this kind of work a million times before. She

knew how to look at sensitive information on someone's personal laptop. She was just going to pretend this laptop wasn't hers.

Lucca isolated the laptop. For the moment, it didn't have to be attached to any internet connection; she had already downloaded the email.

Then she tugged her robe tightly closed, leaned forward, and opened her email program.

There were more of those grief spam emails than she had thought. Before she even opened them, she glanced at who had sent them. She didn't recognize the name on the account, but the actual address used to send the email had a dodgy URL. She didn't go there. She had another system she would use for that, or maybe, if things weren't as bad as she feared, she would report the URL to the office, and let her staff work on this.

She paused over the Rob-specific emails. There were at least a dozen of them, maybe more if she checked her spam filter, which she wasn't ready to do yet. Whoever had set up the subject line had done so with care, so that the emails *wouldn't* get caught in the spam filter.

Her hesitation was not unusual. She needed to figure out how best to deal with these emails.

But if she had been opening the emails in real time, rather than ignoring her personal laptop altogether, she would have opened a few one day, and more the next.

So the best thing she could do was open these emails in chronological order.

She let out a small breath. Whoever had sent these emails had waited more than a week for her to open them, and then, when she hadn't, had sent email to her daughters.

Had she not been an investigator, she would have immediately thought that all of this was personal. But her daughters were listed in the obituary, and anyone with a computer and the sense of a half-wit could find them.

Lucca's mouth was dry, and she wished she had grabbed her coffee. But she hadn't. Then she clicked on the first email—received a day or so (maybe hours) after the obituary was published.

The Truth About Robert Zedder! The interior screamed, just like a headline.

Then it quoted the obituary—loving father and husband—with several attached pictures underneath the words.

The pictures were what she expected. Blurry images of a man who might or might not be Rob, kissing a woman who was definitely not Lucca.

Lucca could fake up this sort of thing in less than fifteen minutes. She could search for the images on the internet and see where they were pulled from, and maybe even identify the couple.

But she didn't.

Instead, she opened the next email.

It had a subject line similar to the one she had just looked at, and the format was the same. Only this one was focused on "loving father." Again, blurry photos, clearly obscene and awful, with a man and a girl who couldn't have been more than eight.

The man might've been Rob. But he might've been any other dark-haired middle-aged tubby white guy.

This stuff was generic, disgusting and hideous, designed to upset the recipient. But Lucca had seen worse, much worse, from people she had thought she had known. Those upset her.

This was a poor attempt at—what, exactly?

She couldn't find anything that stated a purpose in the email. Not a link, not a request for money, not a claim of blackmail, nothing.

It looked like someone was trying to destroy Rob's reputation, but surely, anyone who would want to do that would know that Rob's wife was a private investigator and would be able to figure out who had sent the emails.

Or maybe it was some kid at the high school who had hated Rob, and decided to get revenge on his family.

Lucca let out a small breath. That thought made her feel a little unclean. It would take a special kind of budding young sociopath to come up with something like this.

But this could be an entire blackmail campaign, with the ask at the end. The fact that there were a dozen or more of these things led her to believe that inside these emails would be some kind of escalation—she just wasn't sure what it would be.

She backed up her email program and all of the emails on two different thumb drives, just in case opening one of the other emails would destroy her entire computer. Such things happened a lot to her clients, and her team was usually called in too late to deal with the mess.

While the program was copying onto the thumb drives, Lucca used time to take a quick shower (first time in two days!), put on the jeans and denim shirt she had laid out the night before, heat up some coffee, and grab one of the chocolate banana muffins someone had given her.

The orgy of food had been amazing right after Rob's death, and Lucca had expected it to slow down, but since she wasn't communicating (much) with her friends, they had taken to leaving food baskets on her doorstep.

People were worried about her, and she found that both touching and irritating and, at the moment, highly convenient.

She walked back into the inner sanctum just as the laptop bonged its little *I'm done!* sound. She pulled the thumb drives and labeled them, setting them near her phone as something to deal with later.

Her phone's screen flared on, showing four more texts from her daughters, getting more and more insistent.

Lucca couldn't ignore them, not with the girls so very upset. So, she sent a group text to all three of them, telling them to calm down—she had this—and then went back to work.

The next two emails were just as generic as the first two. Then the tone of the emails changed.

See What Rob Zedder Did In The Days Before His Death! emails actually had photographs of Rob, taken primarily off security cameras from convenience stores, traffic cameras, and bank systems.

She felt a flash of irritated responsibility—she was going to have to let all of those organizations know they had been compromised.

Then she sipped her coffee, which was already tepid, crammed part of the banana muffin into her mouth (more chocolate than banana, and good), and looked at the first *What Rob Did* email more closely, to see why the anonymous emailer thought these would be upsetting.

She couldn't see anything upsetting, even when she made the emails larger. She didn't click on the photographs, though.

She would click links and photographs after she had finished the initial glance at the emails.

She was about to give up on that particular series of emails when she figured out what was wrong: the time stamps on each photo—and they all had time stamps, because they were from security cameras—were in the middle of the day, when Rob was supposed to be at the high school.

Her first inclination—her investigator's inclination—was to call the school to see if Rob had actually been at work at those times on those days. But that could wait. Because she still didn't know the purpose of these emails, and she didn't want to be manipulated into any kind of unusual behavior.

The next three emails were simple threats with varying degrees of menace. The upshot of each? *We have more information on Robert Zedder* and the implication was that they would release that information, ruin Rob's reputation, and destroy everyone's belief in him.

But for what gain? She couldn't find that, not yet.

That was beginning to bother her.

Finally, she got to the last three emails. They all had the subject header *Discover Who Robert Zedder Really Was*, but the headline in each email was different.

The first said, *You Think You Knew Robert Zedder. You Were Wrong.*

Buried into the body of the email were more pictures. Only these were screen shots. The first series appeared to be screen shots from SnapChat on someone's phone. The snippet of conversation, from almost a month ago, would have been disappeared by now—stuff remained on Snapchat for only twenty-four hours or so—but someone had thought to preserve it.

And augment it.

One of the handles—midfindotdlegercom—had a computer-drawn fake-handwritten scrawl next to it, identifying it as Rob's. The posts were nasty, vicious, hate-filled, calling out someone for being transgender. Lucca wouldn't have believed it was Rob at all, except that she recognized the handle.

Rob loved using parts of words in a patterned repeat. He had taught her that trick back in the days when passwords didn't need numbers and punctuation. This particular handle came from the words *Middle Finger Dot Com*. (*Mid-Fin-Dot-Dle-Ger-Com*).

Her phone vibrated across the desk. She glanced at the laptop's clock, realized she'd been working for nearly two hours. That call had to be from one of her daughters.

Lucca picked up the phone, glanced at the screen, but didn't answer. The caller had been Marla this time.

I'm still working on it, Lucca texted all three of them. She didn't tell them she had only just gotten to the screenshots.

Given Antoinette's text earlier that morning, the three girls suspected these messages were from Rob as well. He had probably taught them the same trick that he had taught Lucca.

She made herself focus, rather than think about how her daughters were feeling. Right now, they were just clients, and she was going to treat them that way.

Treating them that way enabled her to keep her distance from this, so that she didn't think about her husband, Rob. Instead, she was focusing on some guy named Rob, who might or might not have been a pig on Snapchat.

Although the screenshots weren't just from Snapchat, but from other apps that provided "privacy," deleting messages some time after they were posted. There were even a few screenshots from Facebook's Messenger app, the special feature that also made messages disappear.

And none of the posts were nice. All of them were nasty, trollish, horrid pieces—taking apart gays, African-Americans, and women. Vicious, hideous stuff, the kind of things that Rob The Saintly would have told her that he didn't want "his kids" saying in school.

With some trepidation, Lucca opened the last email.

She had expected some kind of ask or a request to go to a website or a demand for money so none of this would go out.

And there was none.

Just two sentences:

Aren't you happy to be rid of that asshole now? You really should thank me.

And then, nothing.

Nothing at all.

———

She had to stand up after reading those two lines. She grabbed the last part of the muffin, ate it without really thinking about it, and chased it with the remains of the coffee.

Then she went into the kitchen to get more.

She was fully aware that she was dealing with her sudden stress by shoving it down with food. Which was better than what she had been doing all week, which had been avoiding food, except when her body reminded her.

She grabbed another chocolate-banana muffin, poured more coffee, thought for a brief minute about actually putting something healthy in her body, and then decided against it.

She was working. It shouldn't matter that she was working on something about Rob. She needed to act as if she hadn't met him at all.

Although, if she hadn't met him, she would think he had written all of that crap in the screenshots. She might even consider that he had done the stuff in the blurry photos.

She shuddered. If she had spent years sharing her bed—her life—with a creature like the one in "loving father" then she should be indicted herself.

She didn't even remember sitting down in her leather chair. One moment she was in the kitchen, the next she was checking her spam filter. There had to be an ask, somewhere. Or a demand. Something to make this effort worthwhile to the sender.

She didn't find it in the spam filter or in the junk folder. She checked through the email again to see if she had missed something.

She hadn't.

Could it be that the person who had sent these emails hadn't wanted a response from her? Had they sent emails to her daughters because the barrage that came to Lucca was done? Were they trying to convince the family that Rob wasn't the person they had thought he was?

Lucca stood, remembering Antoinette's voice, shaking like it had when she was six. Seeing the texts from all three of her daughters: *Mom, those screenshots aren't real. Are they?*

Already the doubt. Already the worry.

Some poison had wormed its way into Lucca's family—and she wasn't sure how to get it out.

———

First things, first, though. She had to find out what her daughters had received. She texted them, telling them to forward the emails to her personal laptop account rather than any business account, like she would have if they were clients.

She figured the laptop account was already compromised —hell the laptop itself might've been compromised—so she was just trying to contain the problem into one space.

Besides, she was trying to act like a client would. If someone was monitoring the online communications—as Rob's wife, not as Lucca Kwindale, private investigator—they would expect the daughters to forward their emails. A healthy family would work together, and Lucca's family had been healthy.

Hadn't it?

She rubbed a hand over her face. It would be so easy to blame the grief or the exhaustion on her emotional roller coaster, but that wasn't entirely why she was having doubts.

There had always been parts of Rob she hadn't understood, and as he had gotten older, parts she hadn't liked. They were a true mismatch, the kind that happened when people got married too young.

She hadn't left because of the girls, although she had been toying with it now that Antoinette was nearly out of college. The household hadn't had to remain stable, she had been thinking, and she had seen no reason to live in the big house with a man she wasn't really sure she would have talked to if they had met now.

Lucca gathered the crumbs of the second muffin, not remembering consuming all of it. She dribbled them into her mouth like a teenager.

She had been dealing with those thoughts—the thoughts of divorce, of leaving—ever since Rob had died. She hadn't told anyone about that, not because she felt guilty, but because she didn't.

Maybe that was why the doubts had come so fast. She hadn't liked him, not the man he had become.

But it was a stretch to think he had skipped out of work and even more of a stretch to think he had written all of those nasty things on all of those social media sites.

She wiped off her fingers, sipped even more coffee, and went back to work. She had a moment of trepidation as she attached the laptop to her dedicated internet line. She half expected the laptop to freeze up, or ransom ware to appear, but nothing like that happened.

She downloaded the email, then immediately went offline. She would do the other work—going to the websites and links —later, depending on what she found.

She isolated her daughters' emails by daughter, wondering if they got different emails. Lucca started with Marla's because she was the eldest. She was also the most visible of the children, and ostensibly, the one with the most money. If Lucca were doing this horrid thing, she would have gone to the wife first, and then getting no response, to the eldest child, and worked her way down.

But if Lucca had been doing this horrid thing, she would have asked for money to keep the damn information off the streets, rather than sending that pointed final email.

The emails weren't quite the same. First, Marla hadn't received all twelve. She had only received seven—although Lucca would ask her to double-check her spam filters.

The first three were exactly the same, including the hideous "loving father" email. There was only one in the middle, with photos showing Rob coming out of a hotel, photos taken by the security camera of a bank. Lucca had received those photos as well.

The last three were different, though. They were screenshots, yes, but they were from private chat boards. The handle was the same as on the ones she received— midfindotdlegercom—and Rob's name had been "written" in the same red lettering as on her screenshots.

But these were worse than Lucca's. Not in political content, but in personal content. They would dig directly into Marla's self-esteem.

I got "blessed" with three daughters, one of the posts read, *and all of them take after my wife, who is no prize, let me tell you. I was happy to have married the oldest daughter off, because she made bitchiness her life's work. Couldn't wait for her to move out.*

And another:

Don't get your girlfriend pregnant, no matter what you do. If I'd used a condom, I wouldn't have been "blessed" with the Bitch Queen of the Universe as a daughter.

Lucca took her hands off the keyboard. She stepped away from the laptop, because if she didn't, she would put her fist through the screen.

Those posts were Rob's. She knew it as clearly as if she had heard him say those things.

One of his favorite sayings was "Bitch Queen of the Universe," only he'd used it to describe a woman he worked with, as well as the Watersville's mayor. Lucca had never heard him use it to describe his daughters, though. Although he hadn't really liked Marla.

He'd said that to Lucca many times over the years, always

in a perplexed way. *Isn't a father supposed to fall in love with his child?* he'd ask.

The question was plaintive in the beginning, then biting later. He'd actually talked about getting a DNA test when Marla was thirteen and difficult. The subtext was—always had been with her—that she was Lucca's fault.

Lucca, for not being on the pill. Lucca, for refusing to terminate the pregnancy. Lucca, for trapping him into marriage—even though he had been the one to ask her. She had told him, more than once, that she was perfectly willing to raise the baby alone.

And that was the thing that bothered her the most. Only two people knew that Lucca had been pregnant when she got married. They hadn't lived near family at the time, so they had "eloped," going to Vegas for a quickie wedding.

She had been four months pregnant, but not showing from the angles of the photographs they had taken. That had been July. Marla had been born in December. And with her birth announcement, they had included the announcement of their marriage, changing the date so that it seemed like they had gotten married in March instead.

Her parents had been wounded that Lucca hadn't had a traditional wedding, but they had known that their middle child had never been a traditional person. His parents were crushed, and that was when the blaming had started.

If only I had worn a condom, he would say until finally Lucca had shushed him.

You keep saying that and when the baby gets older, she'll have a complex, Lucca said.

She had been a young twenty-four when she married him, still naïve enough to believe that two parents were better than one, idealistic enough to think that love (even pallid love, like theirs) would survive anything, hopeful enough to believe that a second child would make things better, and tired enough to figure out that a third child wouldn't make that much difference—especially when she, like her oldest sister, hadn't been planned.

Lucca glanced at her phone. No texts now, except one from her office.

Call when you're feeling up to it, her office manager wrote.

Lucca certainly wasn't feeling up to it at the moment. If she talked to anyone, she'd bite their head off.

She sat back down.

Time to find out if her other daughters had gotten similar emails.

Time to find out exactly what the hell was going on here.

———————

Both Sybil and Antoinette had received seven emails, and four of them were exactly the same as the ones Marla and Lucca had received. But the last three were different in each case, personal, and nasty.

And clearly written by Rob.

The things he had written about Sybil and the fact that she had embraced the traditional values of her husband were breathtakingly vicious. Compound that with the slurs Rob wrote about Sybil's conversion to Catholicism, and the devastation was complete.

Lucca's heart ached for her daughter, who didn't deserve any of that, no matter how holier-than-thou she had gotten when Rob confronted her years ago.

He hadn't liked any religion, not deep down.

Maybe Lucca should have had that religious funeral after all, not as a sop to Sybil, but as a fuck-you to Rob.

If only Lucca could do it all over again.

She hesitated before opening Antoinette's emails. Sybil and Marla were women full-grown, and they had their own families who loved them, and could help them through this.

But Antoinette had just broken up with her girlfriend, and had had to move out just the week before Rob died. Antoinette had been fragile then, losing a love she had thought would be permanent.

Lucca couldn't quite imagine how her daughter felt now.

Particularly since half the stuff Rob had said about her had been ugly too. The homophobic slurs that Lucca had received in her three emails appeared in Antoinette's emails, and they seemed worse, because they were actually combined with some kind of weird empathy.

I got a butch daughter, one of the comments read. *She's perfect except for her predilections. I'd thought she was the daughter of my dreams until I realized she had this flaw. I know without asking that the bitch-wife won't tolerate any kind of conversion therapy, so we gotta live with a near-perfect child who is going to destroy her entire future by either being too butch to ever get a high-end job or being too focused on politics to do good work at whatever job she does get.*

Lucca's lower lip trembled. A tear ran down her cheek, but she wasn't mourning anymore. She wasn't grief-angry anymore either. She was sad for her daughters.

Who would do this to them? They didn't need to know how their father had actually felt.

Lucca had known about some of his feelings, but not all of

them. And she had never put them together into such a vile package.

She had no idea what she would say to her girls.

Aren't you happy to be rid of that asshole now? the emails asked.

If it had just been her, yes, she would have been.

But what he had done to their daughters…

Had his attitudes shown up in the way he treated them? Had they already known how he felt?

Probably. Kids weren't stupid.

Adults were.

———

The office was a buzz of activity.

Set in the back corner of a two-story strip mall from the 1960s, Kwindale Investigations took up two-thirds of the lower L. The entry was behind some badly placed stairs. She could have moved the entry to another part of the L, but she didn't. She liked to make the clients work a bit before they hired her.

Three cars were in the parking lot when she pulled in, and all three belonged to her employees. She walked through the front, laptop under her arm. She had spent an inordinate amount of time cleaning herself up—changing out of the jeans and denim shirt, and opting for khakis and a white summer sweater instead.

She wasn't going to look like death warmed over anymore, not for the asshole she had married.

She was aware that the bitterness she felt was, in part, from the emails. The sender had achieved his goal in that, at least.

But not all of it. If she hadn't already been toying with leaving Rob, she would have been a lot more confused, maybe even spiraling deeper into some kind of depression.

Right at the moment, though, depression seemed very far away. What she wanted was to mutilate her husband's corpse and castrate the person who had sent the grief spam to her daughters.

Why she thought the perpetrator was male, she had no idea, but she was convinced of it. And her hunches were almost never wrong.

The office seemed blessedly normal. The windows to the street were shaded, but the reception area was brightly lit thanks to the three sunlamps that her receptionist kept around the desk.

Smaller offices opened off this bigger room, and directly behind the reception area was a conference room with a long Formica table. Usually the table was filled with employees working off company laptops, but occasionally Lucca cleared it for a gigantic meeting with clients.

The office smelled of fresh oranges, which meant it was around 2 in the afternoon—exactly when Cornelius, her very first hire and now her right hand, had his mid-afternoon snack.

Lucca waved at the receptionist who started to ask how she was. Lucca pretended she didn't hear, opened the door to Cornelius's office without asking, and stepped inside.

He was a big man with a close-cropped afro. He favored loose clothing—today's shirt was a white-and-tan weave that looked like expensive "local" sourced material, just the kind of politically correct clothing he preferred. His gym bag was half open against the far wall, some sweat-stained clothes hanging out of it.

He stood as she came in.

"Lucca," he said in his deep George-accented voice. "I didn't expect you."

"Said I might be in today." She set the laptop on his desk.

"Yeah, but when you didn't return my call earlier, I figured you weren't coming." He frowned down at the laptop.

"I didn't even listen to the message," she said. "I need you on a case."

His eyes narrowed. She never said things like that—not anymore. Now, he brought in his own cases, just like she did.

"That's your computer," he said.

She nodded. It hadn't taken much for him to deduce that. She had stickers across the top of the laptop marking it as *Property of Lucca.* She had learned that the hard way, when she had accidentally opened a client's laptop thinking it was hers.

"The girls and I are being targeted by a spammer," she said. "I need you to find out who it is. I also need you to look at the photos in the early emails and see if they're just generic internet images, blurred, or if they're actually what they purport to be."

Cornelius slid the laptop to his side of the desk, then rested his fingertips on top of it.

"About that, Lucca," he said.

She frowned. "About what, exactly? I need you on the job. I don't want anyone else to see this—"

"No," he said. "About the spammer."

His expression was serious. He paused just long enough for her breath to catch.

"You got some spam too," she said.

"No," he said, "actually, we didn't. But the school district called. They got quite a bit, and they wanted us—they wanted me, specifically—to see if it was legit."

Lucca's cheeks heated. "Spam about Rob?"

Cornelius nodded.

"In email?" she asked.

He nodded again.

"When did it start showing up?" she asked.

"Right after he died," Cornelius said. "That morning, in fact."

She frowned. She hadn't expected that. The school district had gotten email before she had, which changed the focus of everything.

"What kind of email?" she asked.

"To tell the truth about Rob," Cornelius said.

"Pictures of affairs, and child abuse, and screen shots from chat rooms?"

Cornelius actually leaned back just a little. His face didn't register surprise, but his body did.

"No," he said. "Financial records."

She blinked, unprepared for that. "What kind of financial records?"

"The hacked kind," Cornelius said. "Rob's financial records."

"And mine?" she asked.

Cornelius shook his head. "Just his, from one local bank and two online banks."

"Online banks?" she asked. "We don't bank at online banks."

"I know," Cornelius said quietly. Everyone who worked at

Kwindale Investigations knew what she thought of online bank security for some of those new start-up banks.

Rob had known that too.

"Rob had accounts of his own?" she asked.

Cornelius nodded again. It was almost as if he wanted her to make some kind of leap on her own.

"With what money?" she asked. "His paycheck was direct deposited into our joint account."

"He started the accounts with the school district's money," Cornelius said softly.

It took her a moment to connect the dots. Five years ago, Rob had been temporary treasurer for the school district when the original treasurer had been fired for cause. Rob had repaired the books, and had gotten them ready for a forensic accountant. Or so he said.

"Rob was the one embezzling?" Lucca asked. "Not that woman who got fired?"

"Oh, they both were, just at different times." Cornelius's fingers tapped Lucca's laptop. "He just took her ideas and improved on them."

For the second time that day, Lucca's knees gave out. She sat in the closest chair, a wooden thing without a cushion at all.

"And no one noticed money was still disappearing?" she asked.

"A lot of money went missing the first time," Cornelius said. "Or rather, Rob's reports said a lot of money went missing. He postulated there was one account that still had school district funds draining into it, but no one could find the fund."

"Because it was his," she said.

Cornelius didn't even bother to nod this time. He just watched her as if he expected her to burst into tears.

She was long past tears. She was long past anger. She had moved into an emotional space she had never occupied before. It was a kind of calm that felt powerful, as if it had a lot of energy behind it.

"How long have you been working on this?" she asked.

"Long enough to know I needed to notify you before you met with an attorney to help you with Rob's estate," Cornelius said.

She hadn't yet found an attorney. There had been no hurry because, under state law, everything passed directly to her. She had wanted to use Rob's death to put her own finances in order, to make sure the girls were cared for in a way that *she* wanted, not the ways that Rob had suggested.

The bastard.

Lucca let out a breath. When she had gone to an attorney and done a search of everything, she would have found these accounts. If she had waited a long time, it might have been hard to prove she hadn't known about them.

Embezzling. She hadn't expected it. But then, she hadn't expected any of this.

"How much are we talking?" Lucca asked, surprised her voice sounded as calm as it did.

"Enough that it puts him into the WTF category," Cornelius said.

It worried her that he didn't give her an amount. Although she had an idea from what he said. The WTF category was one they used in the office for the truly stupid, usually spouses who cheated on their partners and were blatant about it.

But with financial crimes, the WTF category was even more

what-the-fuck. Kwindale Investigations (particularly Lucca and Cornelius) saved WTF on financial crimes for the person who had stolen or embezzled a boatload of money, and should have shipped the funds to one of those banks that kept no records, and then the person should have run off to a country with no extradition.

Doing it this way was just a guarantee that the person would eventually be caught.

Lucca rubbed a hand over her face, thinking about it all, thinking about Rob, wondering why he had become that man.

She had no answers.

"You're sure he did this," she said.

Cornelius nodded. "Our lovely hacker sent hundreds of emails of your husband in the one bank, and we could focus down on some of the forms he was filling out. He had the right account numbers."

Hundreds of emails. Lucca and the girls only had a few.

Lucca didn't say anything. She was trying to get her brain to function faster, but it was still stuck in grief mode.

"We've had two weeks to investigate this, Lucca," Cornelius said gently. "We're sure it was him."

She nodded. She had only had hours to investigate the grief spam she had received, and she was certain that the most harmful posts had been his as well.

"Do you know who is doing this?" she asked.

Cornelius sat down at his desk, putting it between him and her. He used to put furniture between them when he was a new hire, afraid she would get angry at him.

She never got that kind of angry, although she often made him redo a lot of his work, back in those days.

He was so far past redoing anything, so far past needing supervision, that she trusted every word he had said.

Of course, she had trusted Rob too—or had she? She had handled the family finances for years. Rob had been on a budget that they both set. She had kept to her budget too, except for her business. And all of the money she had earned at her business had gone back into her accounts.

He couldn't touch it.

Her famous hunches—she hadn't been paying attention to them when it came to her husband.

But to be fair to herself, he had been grandfathered in. He had been around before her hunches were something she trusted.

What had she said once about a client? That the woman had been a frog in a pan of cold water. The frog hadn't noticed that the water was heating up, until it was too late.

She had been that goddamn frog. How had she become that goddamn frog?

"Lucca?" Cornelius said.

She blinked, realizing he had been talking and she hadn't heard him.

"I'm sorry," she said. "Tell me again."

He bit his lower lip. "We've been focused on the embezzlement."

He didn't say anything more. He had been saying more when he had spoken the first time.

But he didn't need to say more. The client was the school district, and the school district had just discovered a major crime. Who had alerted them to that crime mattered less than the crime itself.

Lucca reached for the laptop. "You've got your hands full," she said. "I'll take care of this."

Cornelius's fingertips still rested on the silver surface, near Lucca's name.

"No," he said. "We have the resources here. We'll take care of it."

"I'm not sitting at home anymore," she said.

He frowned at her, then sighed. "Take care of the girls," he said.

"I will," she said. "And one way I will is to shut this asshole down."

Cornelius nodded. "I agree. That's important," he said. "But you can't be involved in this."

"I'm not a victim," Lucca said. "I can do this."

"But, Lucca," Cornelius said gently. "You are."

That rage she had been sitting on engulfed her. It took all of her strength to block the next words out of her mouth.

I am not, she would have said to him. *I am clearheaded and ready to work. I need to work. I need to catch this guy. I need to feel...*

Useful.

The word caught her, defused the rage, and made her tear up.

Cornelius didn't see the fight she was having internally. He was saying, "We're going to have to go to court and give testimony on this case, since we found the embezzlement thanks to this guy. We can't have you in the middle of all of that, Lucca. You're going to have to deal with the legal ramifications. These crimes have had an impact on you, whether you want to acknowledge that or not."

The crimes have had an impact on you. The words she had

designed to convince victims who hated the word to accept that someone had hurt them.

"What can I do?" she asked.

"Let us track him down," Cornelius said. "And then we'll figure that out."

———————

After Lucca left Cornelius, she went to her private office. It was neater than her home office. The desk was empty except for her computer, and the files she'd been working on—the paper files—were nowhere to be seen.

She had abandoned a dozen investigations in progress when Rob died, and she hadn't given them a second thought until now. Cornelius had clearly stepped in and taken over. She opened the computer, saw that he had assigned the cases that were nearly finished to the newest investigators, and gave the rest to the more experienced investigators.

Normally, he probably would have kept one or two for himself, but he hadn't, which told her how all-encompassing this investigation for the school district had been.

She sat down, and rubbed a hand over her face. She was tired. Not physically tired. Emotionally tired. She'd probably experienced every negative emotion possible so far today, and she would probably experience a few more before the day was out.

Starting with the emotions that were coming in the next few minutes.

She texted her daughters jointly and asked if she could set up a video conference. She would rather be discussing all of this with them in person, but everyone lived in different cities.

She had already toyed with the idea of telling the girls what she had learned later, when the investigations were done, but that would leave them with the uncertainty and the pain of those posts Rob had completed.

Better to rip off the Band-Aid quickly, as she had learned in her first few years of mothering. Sparing a child pain by not telling her something, or by telling it slowly, usually compounded the pain.

And this pain—thank you, Rob, you asshole—was impossible to ignore.

The girls were all available now for a video conference, and she braced herself. The last thing she wanted to do was tell her daughters that everything was true, and that there were even worse accusations.

But she was going to.

The call went through, and one by one, her daughters appeared on her computer screen. Marla had her curly hair pulled back, her face gray, and the shadows under her eyes deep. She looked like she hadn't slept in days.

Sybil wore a black blazer that accented her broad shoulders. A gold cross glinted on the Peter Pan collar of her black blouse. The color suited her, and gave her cheeks color, but her eyes resembled Marla's—sunken and haunted.

Antoinette's short black hair hadn't even been combed that day, or if her hair had been, she had run her fingers through it so many times it stuck out haphazardly around her face. Surprisingly, though, her eyes were dry. In them, Lucca saw a reflection of her own. Antoinette's voice hadn't shaken with unshed tears this morning; it had shaken with complete fury.

Lucca had forgotten that side of her youngest: when Antoinette got hurt, she rose up in righteous wrath, ready to do battle. She had even done so that day long ago when she'd broken her leg. Lucca had had to stop Antoinette from hitting the tree with her tiny little fists.

"It's true," Antoinette said tightly before anyone else could even say hello. "All of it. It's true."

"I don't know about all of it," Lucca said. She fell into a tone that she hadn't used in years—Reasonable Mom Voice. It said *This is awful, but I'm going to be calm, so you be calm too.* "But the screenshots, from what I can tell, they were written by your dad."

The girls all started talking at once. Angry, vengeful, tear-filled, horrified. And then Sybil burst into shaking gulping sobs, and all three of the others tried to comfort her from far away.

It was at that point that Lucca realized this wasn't a one phone call kinda thing. She was going to have to work with her girls on this horrid mess Rob had left them with every single day, maybe more than once.

Cornelius had been right: she was too close emotionally to do any of the fine computer work. Her computer work was going to have to be with her daughters, her friends, her colleagues—everyone who had known Rob, or thought they had.

Aren't you happy to be rid of that asshole now? The final email—all of the final emails—had read. *You really should thank me.*

Thank me.

As she talked to her daughters, as she listened to their pain, those last two words rolled around in her mind.

She wasn't going to thank whoever did this when she found out who it was. She really was going to eviscerate that person. Because her daughters hadn't needed to know any of this about their father. They could have blithely continued with their lives, feeling ambivalent about him, as Antoinette was saying right now ("I kinda knew he didn't like my choices, but I didn't realize…").

The jerk who had done this had taken any delusions her daughters had had away from them. And he wanted *credit*.

Which meant he wanted to be caught.

Something niggled in her mind at that.

"Mom?" Marla said. "You okay? Mom?"

Lucca blinked, focused, saw all of her daughters looking at their cameras, trying to see through their screens into hers. She wondered what she looked like. Probably as discombobulated as they did.

"No," she said. "I'm not okay. But I'm better than I was yesterday. I have a mission now. I'm going to figure this out for all of us."

When she was done with this call, though, she'd call each of her daughters individually, see if they needed her to come visit. Because she had broad shoulders, just like Sybil. Besides, part of her had divorced Rob emotionally years ago.

The girls were dealing with the loss of their father in two ways: they were dealing with his physical loss, and the loss of the man they had thought they knew.

Aren't you happy to be rid of that asshole now? You really should thank me.

Those words…

Lucca's brain caught the thought that had been niggling, held it, and let her examine it.

This guy, he was bragging. Not about the revelation.

About getting rid of Rob.

"Mom?" Sybil asked, her question sharp. "What are you thinking?"

Lucca made herself smile, knowing the smile was bitter and ironic, and not entirely caring.

"Oh, honey," she said in that Mom voice. "You really don't want to know."

———

When the most painful call of her life was finally over, Lucca stood. She was shaking. She had been emotionally drained before the call, and the conversation hadn't helped that—or the guilt. She should have seen what her husband had become.

Or maybe she should have seen what he was.

She could make all the excuses she wanted, but she was a woman who had prided herself on her ability to read people, and the one person in her life that she was (in theory) closest to was the one she had misread completely.

Which made her question whether or not she had misread others along the way.

She made herself take a deep breath. Now was not the time to doubt herself. She needed to be strong, for the girls—and for herself. She needed to figure out what happened.

She shut down the computer, then paced the small space between the desk and the door.

The police had assumed that Rob had been in a single-car crash. He was a respected high school principal, slightly tubby, middle-aged, a perfect candidate for a heart attack while driving or for a stroke. He might have fallen asleep at the wheel, the police officer who had called her had said, or maybe he had simply missed the corner in the dark.

Nothing unusual in their line of work, or so the police thought.

Because they hadn't known about the double life, about the embezzlement. About the person who had been watching and photographing Rob. Or who had been stealing photographs from security cameras.

The police hadn't known any of that, so they had no reason to investigate the matter further.

You really should thank me.

She owned the car now, or what was left of it. The impound had left a message on her phone a few days ago, asking if she wanted to claim the car. She only had a week or so, they said, to remove any belongings from the trunk or the back seat of the car. If the impound yard had left her that message, that meant there had been items left in the car.

Items that might give her a clue to Rob.

Or to the hacker, the stalker, or whoever he was.

She grabbed her purse, and let herself out of her office, waggling her fingers at Cornelius as she passed his office on the way to the main door.

He frowned at her, mouthed *Are you okay?* She nodded her answer, then let herself outside, stopping for a moment in the bright sunshine.

It seemed incongruous, that sunshine—the opposite of the way she felt. It was a mocking sunshine, rather like the sunshine on 9/11 in New York. The kind of day that should have been perfect, if not for the plume of smoke trailing into the blue, blue sky.

Then Lucca shook her head. Rob had been dead sixteen

days. The 9/11 analogy belonged to Day One, not Day Sixteen. By Day Sixteen, she should have been firmly inside the new reality of life without Rob.

Only Day Sixteen had turned into a brand-new Day One, the day in which she discovered that she had spent decades living a lie.

You really should thank me.

She got into her van, backed out of the small parking area, and drove as carefully as she could to the police impound yard at the north end of Watersville.

She had been to the impound yard dozens, if not hundreds, of times before, always on a case, always looking for whatever it was that someone had left behind.

Like she had almost left things behind. She would have, if she hadn't discovered Rob's perfidy. If the grief spam hadn't tilted her in the right direction.

Although it really wasn't fair to call what she had received grief spam. That had been the casket offers, the avoid-estate-tax directives, and the invest-your-inheritance scams. What she had gotten—what everyone who had been close to Rob had received—had been wake-up emails of a kind that was, in many ways, much worse than the grief spam. Grief spam was impersonal, at least.

This stuff…

She shook it off, trying not to think about her daughters' faces as she had seen them that afternoon. Lucca would look over Rob's car, get her belongings, and if she found nothing, go home.

The impound yard was in the bottom of a hollow about one-hundred yards from the entrance to the dump. During the wettest springs, the impound yard flooded thanks to the intersection of crisscrossing rivers that had given Watersville its name.

Behind the impound yard's chain-link fence, twenty or so cars had been stored as closely together as possible. They were the cars that had been towed here because they were parked illegally or because they had been booted and then abandoned. About half of those cars would get claimed every day, and the rest would eventually get resold at the police department auction.

Behind them, a squat brown building stood. It had enough room for two city employees, one tougher than the other because people sometimes got violent over their cars.

The damaged and destroyed cars, the cars that might be evidence in an actual crime, and the cars that had been stolen (and unclaimed) covered the vast brown dirt between the impound yard and the city dump. She knew from personal experience that some of those cars had sat on the dirt for years, waiting for someone to make a decision about their disposal.

She couldn't see Rob's pride and joy, the stupid red Camaro he had bought without telling her, so soon after Antoinette left for college. They had fought over that stupid car, because Lucca had believed they couldn't afford it. He said he would handle the payment himself, using the money he had out of the family budget for his own discretionary spending.

Since he had done that, she hadn't thought about the damn car again. But now that she knew about Rob's extra accounts, she figured that was what he had been using to pay for the stupid Camaro.

Lucca pulled open the door to the brown building, saw one of the employees—Stu—sitting behind the ancient desk. He stood when he saw her. He was wearing a white T-shirt with a band logo on it, the ridiculous green shirt the city made him wear draped over a chair.

"Hey, Lucca," he said gently. "Sorry about Rob."

She nodded, unwilling to acknowledge that sentence given the mood she was in.

"I hope you're here on a case," Stu said in that same tone.

"You guys called, said there were personal items in the Camaro." She sounded normal—at least, she thought she sounded normal.

"Yeah," Stu said. "I can get them for you. You don't need to see that car."

"Actually," she said, "I do need to see the car."

"Honey," Stu said, "you really don't."

He had never called her "honey" before. The "honey" this time wasn't condescending, just affectionate. His lower lip was turned down a bit, and a frown creased his forehead.

Lucca wasn't going to tell him about the emails or the embezzlement or her suspicions. But she did need to ask him a few questions.

"You ever lose somebody close to you, Stu?" she asked.

"My mom." His frown grew deeper. "Two years ago."

"Then you know how it is," Lucca said. "Sometimes you get an idea in your head and you have to do what you can to get it out of your head."

He took a deep breath, clearly not sure what she was referring to. But she had united them in grief, and that had somehow made him willing to listen.

"The car look unusual to you?" she asked.

His lips got even thinner, as if he were holding back his words. After a pause that was seconds too long, he said, "It was totaled, Lucca, and the interior..."

"I know," she said, although she didn't, exactly. But she had dug through cars whose owners had died inside, sometimes in accidents, and in two instances by gunshot, and she knew that interiors were often filled with blood and brains.

"It's been in the sun," he said.

"I figured," she said.

"You don't need to—"

"Please, Stu," she said. "Answer me. Does the car look unusual to you?"

He closed his eyes as if willing her to go away. But she wasn't going to.

"The dents are wrong," he said, as if she had tortured the phrase out of him. "The back dents. They're all wrong."

————

He led her to the car—he insisted, and she wasn't going to argue.

The Camaro had been dumped in front of a group of cars that were almost unrecognizable as vehicles. They were twisted hunks of black and silver metal, accented by flat tires, popped hoods, and dented car doors. At least the Camaro looked like a car. A ruined car, but a car all the same.

The front end of the Camaro formed an uneven U. The bottom of the U still held the shape of that concrete barrier. She recognized it, had driven by it a million times before Rob's accident, and had always thought of the barrier as a hazard. She hadn't driven by the barrier since, because she knew the Camaro's silver paint would still be scraped along the edges.

She really hadn't expected to see that the Camaro had hugged the barrier. They probably had to use some special equipment to peel it away.

"Did they use the Jaws of Life?" she asked Stu.

He was staring at the vehicle as if it had harmed him personally. "No," he said. "The car wasn't hard to remove. The tires remained intact, so they could just pull it backwards. There've been so many accidents, the tow-truck drivers know how to get vehicles away from that barrier now."

Then he glanced at her to see if that sentence had offended her. It hadn't. Truth rarely offended. It was the lies that hurt.

That thought made her think of her daughters' faces, and tears threatened.

Stu put a hand on her arm. "I told you, this isn't a good idea."

Lucca willed the tears back. "Show me the dents."

As if there weren't enough dents. As if the car wasn't completely destroyed.

He gestured, but her eyes didn't follow quickly enough. They were still riveted to the front of the Camaro, to the windshield, which had bent with the frame, but hadn't shattered. It had spider-webbed instead, and Rob's blood decorated the cracks—black now with two weeks' worth of sunshine and decay.

That thought calmed her. He was gone. He was really and truly gone. Yes, he was still hurting them, but his actions were in the past. They were finite. Once she found out everything he did, she would be able to deal with it.

And, more importantly, she would be able to figure out how to help her daughters deal with it.

Stu looked at Lucca, clearly giving her a moment. "You still want to see it?"

"Sorry," she said.

He gestured again, and this time she watched. She still didn't see what he was gesturing at.

"Just take me over there," she said, and hoped she didn't sound exasperated.

He walked cautiously across the dirt, then crouched beside the Camaro.

"Here," he said, his hand above several deep scrapes on the rear driver's side. "And here." He moved a little closer to the rear bumper.

Rob had bought a black bumper cover for both bumpers, so they "added to the classiness of the vehicle" or so he said. She thought they made little difference.

The bumper cover was torn in three places now because the bumper itself was dented, with small V-shaped dents, spaced oddly along its length.

Rob had been protective of this car. He had come home one afternoon bitching that someone had opened a door and made a dime-sized groove near the gas tank.

He would never have allowed something like these dents.

"You think this happened at the same time?" she asked.

Stu shrugged. "I don't know about the timing of these, or the one on the driver's side," he said. "But look at this."

He moved to the passenger side of the car, and pointed to the rear bumper there.

It took her a moment to realize that the cover remained, hanging by its edges, but the bumper itself was so crumpled that it almost looked flat. It was also silver and blue, which struck her as odd.

She looked over at Stu. He was frowning.

"Think about this." He pointed at the damage in the back. "Here." Then he pointed at the gigantic U in the front of the vehicle. "And there."

She stepped back so she could see both together.

"The bumper stuff wasn't tow-truck damage?" she asked.

"They didn't attach to the bumper," he said. "They put the car on a flatbed."

"Oh." She swallowed. If she had hit the Camaro in that exact spot with a lot of force on the road not too far from the concrete barrier, she could have sent the Camaro into the barrier, in just that way. Rob wouldn't have had time to correct.

She had thought of that scenario often on that bit of road, especially when someone had been tailgating her. She had known just how easy it would have been to get accidentally shoved into that barrier, which was why so many people had been injured there.

"You're saying this was deliberate?" she asked.

"If I were the investigating officer, I'd take a look," Stu said. "The same paint is on both sides and the back end of the car. Had your husband been in an accident with the vehicle before this?"

"No," she said. She had seen the car the morning before the accident. The Camaro's red paint had glistened in the early morning sunlight as Rob had driven off to school—or at least, that was where she had thought he was going. Now, she wasn't sure. Then, she had thought like she had every morning, that Rob was stupid to take his expensive midlife crisis and park it in a spot marked Principal, putting a gigantic target on his toy.

"So this was all new," Stu said.

"Yeah," she said.

"Then someone kept hitting him," Stu said.

"You think they forced him into the barrier?" she asked.

"Dunno that. It would take a crash scene investigator to know for sure and it might be too late to do a great examination. But if your husband was speeding to get away from someone, then looked over his shoulder, and didn't realize quite where he was, he could have driven into that barrier. And honestly, given the way the Camaro's built, he would have had to have been going really fast—way over the speed limit—to do that kind of damage to the vehicle."

She walked around the Camaro. She couldn't quite get to the front, which was fine. The windows on both the passenger and driver's side had cracked from the impact, but not as badly. The rear window was just fine.

But the sides were scraped, and the back was badly damaged. Stu was right; someone had definitely hit this car more than once. And the car wasn't rear-ended the way a car would have been had someone hit it after the accident with the barrier. Then the car would have accordioned. It hadn't.

"Did you tell the police?" Lucca had a hunch she knew the answer, but she asked anyway.

"They had already closed the investigation when they brought the car here," Stu said.

Which was why he could call her and tell her to pick up Rob's things.

"But you could have called them when you saw the damage," she said.

He opened his hands, as if to say *What can I do?* "I had no idea if the damage predated the final accident. I see a lot of stuff, Lucca."

She knew that. Which was why she had trusted him in numerous investigations. He saw things, but he was cautious.

She opened her purse, and rummaged around until she found one of her evidence bags. She pulled it out, along with a small scraper she had bought just for this kind of thing.

Then she walked over to one of the dents, crouched, and scraped some of the blue paint into the bag.

"Lucca," Stu said in a chiding tone. "Tampering with evidence."

"Evidence of what?" she asked. "At this moment, there's no case. And besides, the car's been sitting in the lot for more than two weeks. Anyone could have done this."

"You shouldn't be investigating," Stu said. "He was your husband."

The second person that day to warn her off an investigation. She would have paid attention too, if she had planned to bring charges. But she was just trying to figure out what had happened.

"Call the police when I leave," she said. "Please tell them I had said the car was undamaged the moment of the accident and—"

"And I got a twinge of conscience and felt they should reopen the investigation." He nodded. They had done this dance a few times before, but never on something so personal. "Sure thing, Lucca. As long as you're sure you want this."

Her gaze met his. His blue eyes were clear, but that frown remained.

Did he know something about Rob that she didn't? Oh,

hell. Everyone probably knew something about Rob that she didn't.

"Yes," she said. "I want this. I want this very much."

————

And within the hour, she was back in the inner sanctum. Back when she started as a private detective, she did a lot of work for insurance companies. Often that involved identifying cars from hit-and-run accidents. She had learned a lot of short cuts to identifying paint chips, shortcuts that didn't involve a mass spectrometer or a chromograph.

She had learned long ago that the big forensic science stuff wasn't always necessary. Sometimes she just needed common sense—and the ability to hack into the police department records.

First thing she did was look at stolen car reports for that week in April, isolating blue cars only. She found six cars stolen, and only two had a shade of blue even close to the one she was looking at.

One of those cars had been found. It had been totaled. The police figured someone had taken it on a joyride.

She figured someone had used it to repeatedly slam into Rob's car.

Then she leaned back and stared at the car itself. It was a 2017 sports car with enough horsepower to go after a Camaro, and enough weight to do some damage.

The police report said the interior of the sports car had been wiped clean, which was unusual in a joyride. Usually the joyrider figured that the car was so damaged no one would dust for prints. And usually, the joyrider would be right.

Then she went back to the police report. The car was reported stolen at seven the morning Rob was killed. Four hours after he died.

Police discovered the car two days later at the bottom of an empty culvert about fifteen blocks from where the sports car had supposedly been stolen.

The car's owner lived nowhere near either place. He lived on the south side of Watersville, in one of the many apartment complexes that littered the freeway.

Yet he had called, saying he had come out in the morning to find the car missing. How could he have come out in the morning from his apartment to find the car missing from a completely different address?

The details didn't entirely add up.

She looked at the owner's name. The car was registered in the name of Thomas G. Hedges. Hedges. That name rang a bell.

Thomas Hedges. Tom Hedges. Tommy Hedges.

Yes, indeed. Tommy Hedges. He had gone to Anderson High School. His family had moved to Watersville the year before—something about a high-end divorce. His mother had moved the children to a small town to give them "real life." But Tommy had acted out, and Rob had finally expelled him.

Rob had been obsessed with the entire thing, because the mother had called the school board. It had all escalated and someone—Lucca couldn't remember who—finally took the mother aside and told her to send the boy to some rich kid's boarding school.

Lucca had gone to one of the school board meetings during all of that, and she remembered the mother—too thin and dressed to the nines, an aging trophy wife who had been replaced by another trophy—sobbing, begging the school board to let her boy back in, saying he needed to learn how everyone else lived more than he needed to have a high-end education, despite his computer skills.

That had caught Lucca's attention, because she'd sat through a number of those meetings before, usually as Rob's support, sometimes for clients, and no one had said the quality of the education didn't matter. They had always been urging the Watersville School District to up its game, not implying that its sheer ordinariness was a plus.

But did Lucca remember this right? Had the mother actually said *Despite his computer skills?* Or had Lucca heard that elsewhere?

She moved to a different laptop to search for everything she could find on Tommy Hedges. She felt she had to move to a clean laptop just in case he did have mad computer skills.

Just in case he was the person she was looking for.

He had an online presence—everyone did, so that was no surprise. His Facebook page had been active years ago, but he rarely posted now. He did post images of his apartment a few months ago—a one-bedroom cookie cutter, remodeled a little, but its 1970s roots still showed.

Such a comedown, he wrote. *See what happens when you have to pay for shit yourself?*

His other social media accounts were just as sketchy until she stumbled on his second Twitter handle. It was Former-RichBoy1994, and the invective in it was startling. He wasn't nasty like Rob had been. Tommy Hedges didn't write nasty things about people of color or women or engage in any of those online hatred memes.

Instead, he called out hypocrisy, and blamed the system for

robbing him of his life. He hadn't Tweeted much recently, but the day after Rob died, he Tweeted: *No one gets it. They think he's a goddamn saint.*

And then a day later: *I think I did this all wrong. I think if I don't get recognition, it will destroy me.*

She wondered if it was a confession, or if it had nothing to do with Rob at all, if she was making it all up.

She took her hands off the keys and shut the laptop. Stu's and Cornelius's caution had been right: she wanted someone to be guilty—not of killing Rob, but of hurting her daughters.

Lucca wanted to go after whoever it was so badly she had felt something new within herself: she had felt the willingness to blame someone else, based on almost no evidence at all.

She stood up, took the laptop, and placed it in the closet. Then she walked out of the inner sanctum into the messy outer sanctum.

Once there, she pulled her cell phone out of her pocket and called Cornelius.

"I think I have something for you to look into," she said. "And I think you'd better do it now."

———

After that, things moved both faster and slower than she expected.

Faster: the speed of the investigation into the car. Stu's phone call got the police involved, and since Rob had been well liked, the police decided to take another look.

They found all the discrepancies she found. The physical evidence was nearly overwhelming—all of it, scrapes and paint chips and a direct line from Tommy Hedges to Rob.

Tommy Hedges blamed Rob for everything bad that had happened to him after getting expelled from school. The police found other fake identities, other postings, and could link the young man to Rob's murder with startling ease. There was even traffic camera footage that showed the blue car trailing the Camaro. No footage of the actual hits with the car—clearly Hedges had been too smart for that—but there was enough to make a case against him.

Slower than expected: the embezzlement case against Rob. It looked like the school district would just take the money back, without getting too deep into the mess. Lucca wouldn't face charges, because it was pretty clear she knew nothing about any of it.

And while she found that embarrassing, it was also a relief.

Everything else seemed out of time. Her reactions were slower or swifter, depending. Her conversations with her daughters were awkward and sad.

She tried to book a trip to see Antoinette, but Antoinette claimed she was doing all right—that she had help—and recommended that she see Sybil.

Sybil said her church was helping, and Lucca's presence would just remind her of everything she didn't want to think about.

Marla said she had a therapist, and they were working on it one day at a time. But if Lucca felt like she needed comfort, then she was welcome to come visit.

Lucca wasn't sure she did need comfort. She wasn't sure what she needed.

She still cried too much, but she was no longer certain what she was crying about.

She had to break out of this funk. She was beginning to

think the tears were coming from unexpressed anger—anger at Rob for leaving her with such a mess, for lying, for being a true bastard. And anger at Tommy Hedges for shattering her family with his horrid grief spam.

She couldn't do anything about her anger at Rob, but she could do something about her anger at Tommy.

It would just take a little time to arrange.

———

He was in county jail, because he didn't have enough money for bail and his mother refused to bail him out. But she had provided an expensive lawyer, and they had a strategy, which meant Tommy was not talking to the police.

But Lucca thought he might talk to her.

She didn't ask permission from anyone. She knew it would be denied. The police would worry that she was going to screw up the case; the lawyer probably thought she would be acting on the police's behalf.

She was prepared for this meeting, emotionally and physically. She knew what she could and couldn't get away with. She knew how to handle everything—even if Hedges tried to hurt her.

She had gone in and out of that jail more times than she could count, and the guards there gave her a lot of leeway. She had put away some of the worst criminals in Watersville. She had also gotten a few people out.

And she had always treated everyone who worked in the jail with respect, because she knew they had one of the harder jobs in the county.

The building was a squat 1970s cinderblock. She entered the

way she always did, asked to see Hedges, and was told to wait. No one questioned her being there, no one asked her why she needed to see him. Just noted he hadn't gotten a lot of visitors.

Then she was cleared. She had to meet him in the main visitor's area. A family congregated near one of the bolted down tables on the far side of the room, the three children old enough to know where they were. They were looking around nervously, their parents talking quietly, the woman with her hand on the arm of the youngest as if afraid to let go.

Lucca took a table as far from them as she could get. She nodded at the two guards positioned nearest the doors, then waited.

It didn't take long for them to bring Hedges to her. He looked sallow in the orange short-sleeve jumpsuit, his hair cropped short, his skin blotchy. His gaze focused on her, and his eyes narrowed.

"You think I don't know who you are," he said as he sat down. "You're his wife. Lucca Kwindale."

No guard was close enough to overhear the conversation.

"You want to know why I killed him," Hedges said. "That's what everyone wants to know. Not *if* I killed him. *Why* I killed him."

His arms were flabby and surprisingly for someone of his age, without tattoos. She hadn't said a word so far, just watched him, and he seemed content with that.

"I'm not going to tell you anything about that night," he said. "My lawyer said I shouldn't talk to anyone."

He wanted her to ask why he was talking to her. He wanted her to feel special—look! I'm talking with you when I'm not supposed to—but she wasn't going to play that game.

"I don't care why you killed him," she said, her voice soft and low. "Believe me, I get it."

He raised his thin eyebrows. "You get it. You didn't get anything before. You're one of the dumbest bitches who ever walked. Or you're complicit in everything he did."

She thought she had been prepared for those sentiments, but she hadn't been. They stabbed, hard, because both statements were true.

But she had sat across from prisoners before—she had sat across from guilty people before—and she knew how to keep up the appearance of calm even when she wasn't.

"All I want to know," she said, "is why you sent the emails."

A tiny smile played at the corners of his mouth before he could get control of his face. "Some lawyer send you?"

She shook her head.

"Some prosecutor, to see if I'll talk?"

"If that were the case," she said, "we'd be in a different room, with more privacy, so that they could record everything."

"You probably have one of those tiny cameras on you," he said, arms crossed.

"I can't," she said. "I'm not authorized."

He made a face. She wasn't sure he believed her. He clearly weighed his choices for a moment: did he talk to her, risking a camera recording everything? Or did he walk away, and never find out why she was here?

She let him work it out. He had been obsessed with Rob. Rob was gone and she was all that was left. She was gambling that Hedges would choose to stay for that reason.

"So," Hedges said after a moment, and her heart did a little victory dance. "*You* want to know something."

"Why did you send those emails?" she asked.

"Bothered you, did they?" he asked.

"Yes," she said. "It makes no sense to me. You could have gotten away with everything if you hadn't sent the emails."

His crossed arms tightened, pulling on the jumpsuit. "Criminals are dumb," he said sullenly.

She quietly admired how he said that. He hadn't admitted any guilt at all.

"But you're not," she said. "What was the point? Rob was dead."

Hedges' eyes glittered. She recognized the rage in them; she'd seen it in her own eyes of late.

"He ruined my life," Hedges said so softly she could barely hear him over the echoey conversation across the room.

"I know," she said. "He expelled you from school and that started a spiral."

Hedges slammed his hands on the tabletop, making her jump. "It did *not!*" he shouted.

One of the guards came toward her, but she waved him off. The little family watched, the woman holding the youngest tightly against her as if Lucca had shouted at the little girl.

"That's what ruined you, right?" Lucca asked.

"*God!*" Hedges said. "Don't you *fucking* pay attention? Do I have to send more goddamn emails?"

His anger was a physical force. She could feel each word as if it were a punch.

"He didn't embezzle from you," she said.

"No," Hedges said. "He just fucked me."

"He fucked over everyone," she said.

"No," Hedges said again. "He *fucked* me."

His words rang in the concrete room. One of the children was crying. Now, Lucca wished they had taken the conversation elsewhere.

And she realized at that moment, she had deflected what Hedges was saying, tried not to hear it, would have set it somewhere else if she could.

"That second email," she said. "The images were generic."

"Because your goddamn husband was smart," Hedges said. "No contact in person, no pictures, no kiddie porn on his computer. Believe me, I looked."

Her heart started pounding.

"I had some pictures of my own, though," Hedges said. "Small camera, set up just right. But I kept looking at it. I. Kept. Looking at it. And he saw that, he found it, and *that's* when he expelled me. My mom thought I was acting out."

"You accused him?" Lucca said.

"Yeah," Hedges said. "No one listened. He was so fucking respected in this town."

Lucca's breath caught. That was why the police investigation into the accident moved so fast. They already had a police report from years ago linking Rob and Hedges, but it had been buried, possibly because Hedges was a juvenile, probably because Rob was the principal and above reproach.

Lucca swallowed, astounded at her own unwillingness to see her husband for who he was.

"No one told me," she said quietly.

And no one had even tried. She would have remembered.

"I know," Hedges said. "I found out later. The Old Boy Network buried the thing good and fast. They even convinced my mom I was a problem."

"She defended you," Lucca said, remembering the tearful school board meeting. "She tried to keep you here."

"Yeah, she thought that would be good for me. She thought I was making shit up because I was mad. *She* was the one who did that. She accused my dad of all kinds of crap he had never done." Hedges paused, took a deep breath, then narrowed his eyes. "Got your answers now?"

"No," Lucca said. She folded her arms and rested them on the tabletop. "I understand sending emails to the school board. I understand sending them to me. But to my daughters?"

That last word wobbled. She hadn't been able to hide her anger there.

"They're adults," he said.

"They loved him," Lucca said.

"Really?" he asked. "That asshole? Surely they knew what a jerk he was."

Maybe they had. And maybe they had been pretending, like Lucca had, that Rob was better than he was.

Sometimes losing the delusion was harder than losing the person.

"See?" Hedges said. "You should thank me."

"For what, exactly?" she asked.

His smile grew. "For all of it. For waking you up. For freeing you of him. For making sure he'll never hurt anyone again."

Hedges had just admitted to the murder. Her heart started pounding, hard, but she worked on keeping her expression neutral.

"Did he know it was you in the car?" she asked.

"He knew it was me for months," Hedges said. "Those

emails didn't just come together after the fucker died, you know. He'd been getting them forever."

Rob had been getting more and more nervous. She hadn't really paid a lot of attention.

"What changed?" she asked.

Hedges eyes narrowed. "What do you mean?"

"Emails for months," she said. "And then, one night, you get in your car…"

Hedges laughed. "You don't know, do you? You really don't know."

Her cheeks warmed.

He touched one of his fingers to his own cheek, acknowledging her blush. "You don't know," he said with satisfaction. "He had just bought a condo in Perast."

"Where?" she asked before she could think the question through.

"Montenegro." Hedges' smile was wide. He was enjoying her ignorance. "No extradition."

She frowned. "But I didn't find any plane tickets."

"Because he was looking at charters," Hedges said. "That's how I caught him. Looking at charters. He had such a vast digital footprint. He had no idea I was onto that."

"You found it that night?" she asked, letting her own confusion into her voice. Her sorrow seemed to make him talkative.

"Just before I saw him at the restaurant. With one of the boys from the basketball team. The look on that kid's face—I sent the waiter over, told the kid there was an emergency at home, and then I watched while your husband left. He didn't see me until the first time I hit his car. I turned on the dome light, so he could see my face. And he looked scared."

Funny, she didn't care that Rob had been scared. She didn't care that he had died that night. She didn't care about him at all.

But their daughters—what this man had done—she wasn't going to let them come to a trial. And there would be a trial. Because Lucca had caught him.

He had asked about a camera, and she had lied. She hadn't told him she'd been wearing a small audio recorder disguised as one of the buttons on her collar.

She didn't tell him that. She didn't have to.

Prisoners in the county jail were not accorded the right to privacy unless they were meeting with their attorney, which he most decidedly was not.

She had thought she would feel more elated if she got him to confess.

Instead, she just felt dirty and sad.

"He hurt you," she said.

"Oh, yeah, that son of a bitch," Hedges said.

"But you're the one who has chosen to let that destroy you," she said.

His hands curled into fists. "I thought you might say something like that. I thought about that long and hard. Then I figured I could show you holier-than-thou assholes what it's like to have everything taken from you. I'd show you just how easy it is to get over events that totally destroy everything you've ever known."

She studied him for a minute. Then nodded. He was really smart. He could have chosen another way, no matter how difficult.

He hadn't.

And she saw no point in telling him that.

She stood, signaled the guard to let her out, and watched as the door swung back. She could leave. Hedges couldn't.

By his choice.

She had her answers. She also had a lot of soul searching to do. And daughters to help, in her own way.

She had some changes to make. She wasn't as good a detective as she had thought she was. She wasn't even as good a person as she had thought she was.

She needed to change all of that. And the first step was selling the business to Cornelius. Then she needed to do some work, some investigation—not of bad guys—but of the way people survived trauma like her daughters were going through. Like Hedges had gone through.

"You're just going to bury this, aren't you?" Hedges shouted after her. "Do you know how many lives he ruined?"

She stopped before stepping all the way out. She turned her head so she could just see him over her shoulder, still sitting at that table.

"Not yet," she said. "But I mean to find out."

And she would.

Rob wouldn't have been the kind of man who could handle reparations. But she could.

And she would do it.

She owed the community that much.

She owed her daughters even more.

Maybe she *should* thank Hedges. Because without the grief spam, she would never have known. And her daughters would have had to work out their daddy issues on their own.

Then Hedges smiled at her—a mean and feral smile. No. She wasn't going to thank him.

She wasn't in the mood to thank anyone.

She'd been angry for nearly three weeks now. She'd probably be angry for many, many more.

She would use that anger. Because now she had a focus.

All she needed now was a schedule.

Because schedules had value, Rob. Schedules defeated bad guys.

Even when they were already dead.

NEWSLETTER SIGN-UP
DEAN WESLEY SMITH

Sign up for the Dean Wesley Smith newsletter, and keep up with the latest news, releases and so much more—even the occasional giveaway.

Go to **deanwesleysmith.com.**

Sign up for the WMG Publishing newsletter, too, and get the latest news and releases from all of the WMG authors and lines, including *Pulphouse Fiction Magazine, Smith's Monthly,* and so much more.

To sign up go to **wmgpublishing.com**.

Follow Dean on BookBub

ABOUT THE EDITOR

DEAN WESLEY SMITH

Considered one of the most prolific writers working in modern fiction, with more than 30 million books sold, *USA Today* bestselling writer Dean Wesley Smith published far more than a hundred novels in forty years, and hundreds of short stories across many genres.

At the moment he produces novels in several major series, including the time travel Thunder Mountain novels set in the Old West, the galaxy-spanning Seeders Universe series, the urban fantasy Ghost of a Chance series, a superhero series starring Poker Boy, and a mystery series featuring the retired detectives of the Cold Poker Gang.

His monthly magazine, *Smith's Monthly*, which consists of only his own fiction, premiered in October 2013 and offers readers more than 70,000 words per issue, including a new and original novel every month.

During his career, Dean also wrote a couple dozen *Star Trek* novels, the only two original *Men in Black* novels, Spider-Man and X-Men novels, plus novels set in gaming and television worlds. Writing with his wife Kristine Kathryn Rusch under the name Kathryn Wesley, he wrote the novel for the NBC miniseries The Tenth Kingdom and other books for *Hallmark Hall of Fame* movies.

He wrote novels under dozens of pen names in the worlds

of comic books and movies, including novelizations of almost a dozen films, from *The Final Fantasy* to *Steel* to *Rundown*.

Dean also worked as a fiction editor off and on, starting at Pulphouse Publishing, then at *VB Tech Journal*, then Pocket Books, and now at WMG Publishing, where he and Kristine Kathryn Rusch serve as series editors for the acclaimed *Fiction River* anthology series.

For more information about Dean's books and ongoing projects, please visit his website at www.deanwesley-smith.com and sign up for his newsletter.

For more information:
www.deanwesleysmith.com

facebook.com/deanwsmith3
patreon.com/deanwesleysmith
bookbub.com/authors/dean-wesley-smith